FOOTSTEPS AFTER

THE FALL

DAVID LLOYD STRAUSS

www.FootstepsAfterTheFall.com

A Giggle Yoga Production

www.GiggleYoga.com

Giggle Yoga, LLC
PO Box 28
Boulder, Colorado 80306
www.GiggleYoga.com

For bulk orders, contact us
through our website.

Limited First Edition : January – 2011

ISBN – 13: 978-0-615-43837-5

Book One in the Giggle Yoga Series.

All photographs courtesy of David Lloyd Strauss.

A percentage of profits from this book
will be donated to assist disadvantaged youth.

Graphics and Book Cover

Iluzion Grafix
Michael A. Cordova
www.iluziongrafix.com

Editor: Mark David Gerson

Mark David Gerson is a project consultant/editor, screenwriter, script analyst, writing/creativity coach, artist and photographer and is author of two award-winning books, *The Voice of the Muse: Answering the Call to Write* and *The MoonQuest: A True Fantasy*. For more information on Mark David visit: www.markdavidgerson.com.

Life is the art of drawing without an eraser.

~ *John Gardner*

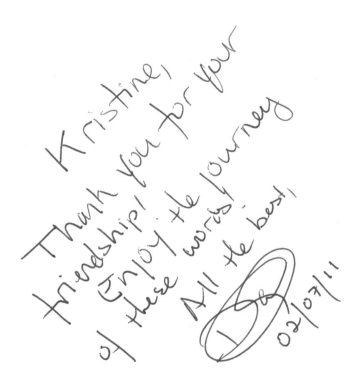

Kristine,
Thank you for your
friendship! Enjoy the journey
of these words.
All the best!
02/07/11

Desiderata

Go placidly amid the noise and
haste and remember what peace
there may be in silence.

As far as possible
without surrender
be on good terms with all persons.

Speak your truth quietly
and clearly;
and listen to others,
even the dull and the ignorant;
they too have their story.

Avoid loud and aggressive persons,
they are vexations to the spirit.
If you compare yourself
with others,
you may become vain and bitter;
for always there will be
greater and lesser persons
than yourself.

Enjoy your achievements
as well as your plans.

Keep interested
in your own career,
however humble; it is a real
possession in the changing
fortunes of time.

Exercise caution
in your business affairs;
for the world is full of trickery.

But let this not blind you
to what virtue there is;
many persons strive for high ideals;
and everywhere life
is full of heroism.

Be yourself.

Especially, do not feign affection.
Neither be cynical about love;
for in the face of all aridity
and disenchantment
it is as perennial as the grass.

Take kindly
the counsel of the years,
gracefully surrendering
the things of youth.

Nurture strength of spirit to shield
you in sudden misfortune.
But do not distress yourself
with dark imaginings.

Many fears are born
of fatigue and loneliness.
Beyond a wholesome discipline,
be gentle with yourself.

You are a child of the universe,
no less than the trees and the stars;
you have a right to be here.
And whether or not
it is clear to you,
no doubt the universe is
unfolding as it should.

Therefore be at peace with God,
whatever you conceive Him to be,
and whatever your
labors and aspirations,
in the noisy confusion of life
keep peace with your soul.

With all its sham, drudgery,
and broken dreams,
it is still a beautiful world.
Be cheerful.
Strive to be happy.

~ *Max Ehrmann*

Table of Contents

Praise the bridge that carried you over.
~ George Colman

I dedicate this book

to everyone who has loved me,

and everyone I have loved –

to everyone who has forgiven me,

and to all whom I have forgiven –

to everyone who has entered my life,

and to all whose lives

I will soon enter.

PROLOGUE:

A Letter To Sunshine

A few minutes ago every tree was excited, bowing to the roaring storm, waving, swirling, tossing their branches in glorious enthusiasm like worship. But though to the outer ear these trees are now silent, their songs never cease.
~ *John Muir*

September 29th, 2010

MY BEAUTIFUL SUNSHINE,

You came into my life like a feather in the wind. You inspired me with your light and renewed my spirit with the gentleness of your love. Words can never express how grateful I am to have you in my life. As I stand here, high atop Hastings Mesa near Telluride, Colorado, all the beauty of Mother Nature reflects the magnificence and purity of your light and love.

I am truly grateful to be here today. This is no ordinary day and no ordinary moment in time. Today is the day I dig deep into my heart and begin completion of the story of a near-death experience that set my life free. The story began on September 7th, 2008, and will continue on for an eternity through the gift of these words. It is here on this mesa during this beautiful moment in time that I am inspired by your beauty to capture the heart and sprit of my magical journey into a world unknown. As I gaze at my surroundings, my eyes are consumed with the beauty of the place I call home. Growing up in Telluride was like growing up in a picture postcard of the most magnificent mountain region imaginable.

During this particular moment, I am on Old Elam Ranch Road, facing south toward my favorite mountain view in the world. The majestic peaks of Mount Wilson, Wilson Peak and El Diente burst up from the floor of the San Juan Mountains with explosive force, parading their beauty for all to see. These three peaks soar more than 14,000 feet into a deep blue sky paraded with only a sprinkling of white, puffy clouds. The landscape is decorated with the lush vegetation of tall aspens, scrub oak and juniper. Greenery as green as the soft petals of a fern dot the field, adding texture and dimension to its quilted form. The entire mesa is blanketed with yellow, blue and red Colorado mountain flowers, and an aromatic bouquet of fresh mountain sage fills the air. It is the perfect setting to find solitude amidst the plentitude of nature, and it's the perfect environment to inscribe my thoughts about life and love and to share the story of my dream, my journey and my awakening.

I arrived on this mesa earlier in the day in the midst of a torrential windstorm. Strong winds pushed across the land, giving a voice to all of nature and wrapping the earth with the cool blanket of an early autumn breeze. One moment was shaded with clouds, while others were filled with the brilliance of light. Everything came alive in the wind. Branches and limbs bent and twisted as unforgiving gusts pressed hard against their tense, rigid form. The air echoed with crackling snaps as weaker limbs gave way to the strength of nature's breath. The sound of aspen blowing in the wind was harmonized by the chorus of their clapping leafs and the splash of water trickling down a stream. All the animals of the mesa — elk, deer, chipmunks, squirrels, rabbits and birds — paused their end-of-summer dances and surrendered the morning to the howling winds.

All is quiet now. The winds have calmed and the silence is only gently disturbed through the shallow breath of the autumn air. The last days of summer are upon us and autumn is beginning to peek through the landscape. A pristine blend of summer and autumn colors abound, painting the face of the landscape with the magic of a change in season. Amidst these colors play the creatures and critters of life's dance of love. Butterflies pass through transparent particles of light, filling the air with their grace, beauty and love, proudly displaying their delicately painted summer wings. A small pond delicately covered with lily pads is surrounded by a bed of moist, green moss topped with a host of summer critters. Gnats, ladybugs and mosquitoes patiently dance upon the splashes of water, cooling themselves in the rising particles of an evaporative mist. As the ants work together bearing twigs and sand, each of the critters goes about its day, living life as it was designed to be lived. Bees dance upon the flowers, and mosquitoes scramble about seeking feed. The smell in the air is fresh as fresh can be. The coolness of moisture and the refreshing scent of rich, green moss are lightly complemented by the beautiful scent of sage and flowers.

Hawks, eagles and crows, the great birds of mountain flight, sailing gracefully through the sky, surfing endless waves of mountain air, pocketing the currents under their soft, feathered wings. Amidst these playful creatures, hummingbirds spin from petal to petal, enjoying the sun-sweet nectar of a flower's free-flowing heart. Chipmunks, cottontails and squirrels rustle amidst the towering flowers and bundles of sage, playing hide-and-go-seek with their siblings and peers.

Rabbits dance to the crinkling sounds of rustling aspens. They twitch their nose, blink their eyes and scratch their ears, as they sense the fluid pulse of the breath of time. They scratch their ears, not out of curiosity, but out of excitement for the freedom to move about in the gaiety of this beautiful mountain landscape.

Time stands still. As I look to the left, two birds dance about in graceful flight, celebrating the beauty of our magical planet. To my right, a deer sips water from a pond, enjoying the afternoon sun and the coolness of refreshing splashes of water on its fur. The deer is completely at peace with the moment, emanating a beauty so natural and so real, that my eyes fill with tears.

The landscape I see and feel is the dream of dreams. Each creature and each piece of nature is a unique expression of an ever changing world, dancing its dance in concert with who and what it is, being what it is designed to be. This colorful palate of images is the canvas of the mystery and magic of life. Whether seen through my eyes, or through the reflection of a dew drop on the petal of a flower, whether imagined or real, these are the colors, eyes and bodies of life and the signature thread of love.

As I stand here, absorbing the endless beauty, I'm overcome with gratitude as I reflect upon the transformational day that rewrote my entire life story and brought me to this grateful moment in time.

Through the beauty and magic of this moment, I offer the words that follow as a gift from my heart, the story of a mystical dream into a cavern of crystals, the story of my journey through ancient ruins, and my collision with destiny that almost cost me my life.

With Giggles, Love and Gratitude,
David Lloyd Strauss

BOOK ONE

*O*ur deepest fear is not that we are inadequate.
Our deepest fear is that we are powerful beyond measure. It is our light, not our darkness, that frightens us most. We ask ourselves, 'Who am I to be brilliant, gorgeous, talented, and famous?' Actually, who are you not to be? You are a child of God. Your playing small does not serve the world. There is nothing enlightened about shrinking so that people won't feel insecure around you. We were born to make manifest the glory of God that is within us. It's not just in some of us; it's in all of us. And when we let our own light shine, we unconsciously give other people permission to do the same. As we are liberated from our own fear, our presence automatically liberates others.

~ Maryanne Williamson

ONE

A Dream Come True

Intense love does not measure, it just gives.
~ *Mother Teresa*

THERE IS SO MUCH BEAUTY to life, yet we never truly appreciate it until time slips between our fingers, and leaves us in the shadow of our memories. I know this to be true because two years ago I almost lost my life, and, by some miracle, I was given a second chance. The sequence of events that led up to and resulted from my renewed opportunity for life taught me many valuable lessons, one of which I will share right now.

If there is anything in life we could ever wish or dream for, it would not be for particular things or experiences. Rather, it would be for the perspective of how wonderful life truly is, because it is through this perspective that we would embrace all that life has to offer, and we would never again waste a single breath or moment.

So often we hear stories of people seeking treasures: treasures of riches, treasures of freedom, treasures of truth, treasures of love. Of all the treasures we seek, though, truth and love are the ones we desire most. We spend much of our lifetime seeking, searching, and hunting for them, never really knowing where to look, yet knowing they're out there. We seek love and truth because we know them to be the most basic part of who we are, and we feel lost not being in touch with our true essence. We experience pure truth and love as young children and, intuitively as adults, we long to experience them again before we die. Through an unexpected turn of events, I found the treasures of truth and love, and it was like nothing that I had ever imagined. I found them through a dream.

Throughout my life I have had a recurring dream about a mystical journey into a cave of crystals. Each time I have this dream, the ending is the same: I am told of a near-death experience that becomes my gateway to understanding truth and love, and the beauty, simplicity and magic of life.

My dream finds me traveling in a make-believe world glistening with the beauty of crystal-like, rainbow reflections. It's an extraordinary dream, a magical moment across the bridge of time, a bridge constructed of crystals woven into a peculiar web humming with light and sound. Each crystal is completely different and carries a harmonic tone unique to its shape and size.

As I cross the bridge, my footsteps are like fingers on the keyboard of a piano. Through the cadence of each step, the harmonic tones of all the crystals are released into an elaborate symphony of angelic music. My footsteps are orchestrated by the music, and my walk turns into an elaborate dance of playful love.

With each movement along the bridge, rainbows of light shower me with the healing power of color. As the light penetrates my body, my skin bursts into a tickling frenzy, leaving my body joyfully electrified, and my skin in a state of exotic laughter. The light is so vibrant that it feels like it is alive. It feels like a joyful life-form of pure happiness and emotional innocence. As the light washes through me, it cradles me in its beauty with the gentleness of a newborn child.

I dance with the light, celebrating the beauty of the moment and realize that each crystal is resonating with the frequency of my thoughts, feelings and emotions. The more energy I put out, the more energy they reflect back to me. With every step forward, I become more and more consumed by the light. My body slowly loses its density and transforms into the energetic essence of pure love and pure consciousness. I enter into a state of blissful surrender and childlike joy. The being of light is now walking with me, through me, as me. It is the light of pure love.

Moving deeper into the heart of the crystals, I discover an astonishing hall of mirrors, a collection of rainbow-colored reflections laid out like a mosaic of tiles, each of which carries stories about the hidden truths of life, the power of the human mind, and the mystical laws of energy that govern our experiences. I study the laws with relaxed intensity. The more I study, the more I learn. The more I learn, the more I grow and, in my growth, I come upon a startling realization that gives me an entirely new perspective on who we are as humans, and on the true depth of our potential.

As I study the laws and reflect upon this realization, one of the crystals begins to pulsate like a beating heart. It draws me closer and closer until a vortex of energy bursts from its center and pulls me, with magnetic force, into a fourth-dimensional sphere...into a loop in time and portal in space through which I am given a deep look into the heart and spirit of humanity. The full palette of human emotions cascades through me like a waterfall of sadness and joy...more and more quickly until the entire sequence begins to resonate a single tone. Then, with a sudden thunderous spark of brilliant white light, I am thrown out of the vortex and back onto the crystal.

The single tone is the collective sound of all the energy that underlies the fabric of life. This energy, which roars into a spark of brilliant light, is the energy of the heart and mind of the entire universe. It is the intelligence of mind and thought, and the heart of love. It leaves me breathless, suspended in emotional awe. The spark of light exposes me to the truth of life and forever alters my perception of reality. It's a truth, which if understood by everyone, would end all suffering, poverty, lack and limitation.

Standing on the bridge of crystals, I realize that the lessons in this dream aren't just for me. They're for me to share with all humanity. It is time for me to wake up, not just from sleep, but from the fears that have kept me asleep.

I raise my arms toward the sky in a posture of total joy and gratitude. A tunnel of light forms around me, its walls a mosaic of energetic buttons that reflect the many possibilities for the remainder of my life. As I scan the buttons, I know the best choice: the one that gives me the most emotional leverage to share the hidden laws with all of humanity.

I close my eyes and silence my thoughts. The wall of light begins to flicker with a warm and soothing rainbow of colors. The brightness penetrates my eyelids and funnels its way through my pupils, creating an internal column of light that cascades downward through my body, penetrating the earth, and upward to the heavens through the crown of my head.

I slowly reach outward into the column, pressing both my hands into it. The column collapses into a dense ball of light and floats into the center of my heart. It then explodes into a giant egg-shaped sphere that envelops my body. A second column of white light passes from the heavens, directly down the center of my body and into the earth. This light feeds the sphere and creates a fountain of energy whose harmonic hum sounds like a chorus of angels. I slowly release my hands to the side of my body. The sphere collapses.

The button I chose in the dream was the journey of learning who we are as humans and what we are capable of...a journey I would experience through my own near death and self-rescue: Within a few months of my most recent experience of this dream, I stepped onto a trail at the ancient ruins of Chaco Canyon, and the dream came true.

TWO

Mountains To Desert

Each blade of grass has its spot on earth whence it draws its life, its strength; and so is man rooted to the land from which he draws his faith together with his life.
~ Joseph Conrad

EVERY ONCE IN A WHILE something happens in our lives that causes us to step back and reevaluate who we are and what we are doing. For me it happened on September 7th, 2008.

It was a beautiful morning in southwestern Colorado. The summer season in Telluride was coming to a close, and autumn was beginning to show her colors. A light dusting of snow painted the peaks, and the coolness of fall chilled the air. The contrast between the approaching winter and the bright orange-and-yellow of autumn redecorated the mountain landscape into a picture-perfect moment in time.

There are many beautiful places on this planet. Yet Telluride, Colorado is breathtaking beyond imagination. Every moment of every day in this mountainous region is pure storybook magic. Perched at an elevation of 8,745 feet, Telluride is neatly tucked away at the end of a sixteen-mile box canyon surrounded by mountains that soar upwards of 14,000 feet. Telluride is one of the few places you can fall in love with over and over again, day after day, year after year. You can taste its beauty with your eyes and lose your mind in the vastness of its magic and splendor. I am deeply grateful for the blessing of having grown up in this community and for the gift of being able to call it my home.

With all the natural magnificence of Telluride, on this day I needed to take a break from my daily life and retreat somewhere other than my precious Shangri-La. Several weeks earlier I had herniated two muscles while training for a bodybuilding show. In five days I would be heading to Denver to have surgery that would put me down for a few months. So a few days of peace, reflection and relaxation was well-deserved.

Though I had a lot of places in mind, my injury severely limited my options. What I really needed was a long reflective drive to a quiet destination where I could easily walk without straining myself. A change in scenery and a different type of beauty would be the perfect retreat. I'm accustomed to the contrast of the mountains: the magic of dense trees, fresh, cool water, and the vibrant, richness of color. Yet what I really wanted was a feeling and landscape that can only be offered through the desert.

There is an ambience and power to the desert that is felt through the eyes. The desert breeds contemplation through visual relief. The stillness of the desert quiets the mind so that you can listen to your heart. The desert offers solitude and a different type of contrast: emptiness and fullness, heat and cold, dryness and moisture, empty space blended with sprinklings of organic life, a single flower smiling amidst the arid vastness, wildlife cloaked behind cactus and sagebrush.

A few hundred miles from Telluride, hidden deep within the heated deserts of northwestern New Mexico, are the remnants of what was once the richest social and ceremonial center of the Anasazi culture. Chaco Canyon is the largest known archeological discovery of ancient ruins north of Mexico, with the most remarkable concentration of kivas (ceremonial rooms) and pueblos in the American Southwest. To this day, Chaco Canyon is still an active part of the sacred culture and ritual of the Pueblo, Hopi and Navajo Indians of the Southwest, many of whom continue to use the site for ceremonies.

The stories about Chaco Canyon's history and spiritual significance are a large part of what drew me there. Ever since I was a child, ancient ruins have been a source of fascination for me. I first discovered the true depth of their beauty and power when I joined my friend David Fitzpatrick on a seven-day vision quest through the Toltec Pyramids of Teotihuacan, Mexico, led by a lady with a heart and soul of diamonds. Cynthia Signet guides vision quests all over the world. Her knowledge and understanding of the many different ancient teachings is what ignited my feverish appetite to explore the many ancient ruins of our planet and to learn and understand their closely guarded secrets to life. I had never been to Chaco Canyon before, yet from what I had been told by Cynthia and others, it was the ideal place to go for a quiet retreat to expand my heart and mind.

While preparing for my four-hour drive to Chaco, I had no idea that later in the day I would have a near-death experience that would completely alter the entire direction of my life.

Even though my destination was Chaco Canyon, the drive from Telluride would be an equally important part of my pilgrimage. I'm a very visual person. When I am looking for answers to questions about life, I usually find them through images in nature or through the lessons of history. This drive is rich with both nature and the history of the pioneering and gold-rush days of the 1800s, each of which would provide plenty of food for thought and a generous serving of inspiration.

The road from Telluride follows the San Juan Skyway, through the San Juan Mountains and Uncompahgre National Forest, through the historical towns of Rico, Dolores and Durango, and onward to the desert. The entire drive covers about 225 miles of luscious, breathtaking mountain views transitioning into spectacular semi desert terrain.

As I left Telluride and said goodbye to the stunning box canyon, I was quickly greeted and energized by the stately beauty of Mount Wilson, Wilson Peak and El Diente. Rising over 14,000 feet above sea level, these three mountains have both claimed lives and given new life to inquiring minds. They are the gatekeepers to the Telluride region. When you first arrive, they fill your mind with awe. When you leave, they kiss your heart with the strength of their beauty. Driving past those peaks was my official farewell...and the beginning of my journey.

I had taken the drive to Durango dozens of times, yet this day was different. Although the reason for my journey was a refreshed heart and a renewed state of mind, thinking about my injury during the drive brought to the surface a deeper struggle that was battling within me. I was feeling lonely and empty inside. With this emptiness, life-altering questions began to fill my heart and mind, and amplified my hunger for a day of solitude.

❖ What can I do with my life that will be meaningful and fulfilling?

❖ How can I create a true sense of purpose and passion?

❖ How do I stop looking back upon the difficult times in my life with fear, and start looking forward with courage and wisdom?

❖ How can I let go of the old thoughts and beliefs that are holding me back from realizing my potential, and how do I replace them with new, empowering beliefs?

Questions are the spark for learning. The questions we ask ourselves influence the direction of our life. If we don't ask clear, well thought out questions, we limit our ability to learn and grow, and we constrain our experiences of life. The inconvenience of an injury pushed me inward and made me more sensitive to my thoughts and feelings, and brought out unresolved curiosities and questions. The anticipation of being laid up for a few months was emotionally agonizing, and also contributed to my elevated level of frustration.

With the Wilson Peaks now disappearing behind me, I entered into sixty miles of spectacular views that are breathtaking in any season. The San Juan Skyway is a seemingly endless collage of crashing waterfalls, dynamic cliffs, peaks, valleys, rivers, dense forest, wildflowers, cows, horses, sheep and wildlife. It was the perfect drive for escaping into my thoughts.

As the road wrapped around the rugged San Juan Mountains, I drove past the entrance to the small town of Ophir and began the upward climb toward the 10,000-foot summit of Lizard Head Pass, named after a rock that looks like the head of a lizard. Once I reached the summit of the pass, I pulled over to take in the beauty and reflect upon the contrast between where I was emotionally and the beauty that surrounded me. How could I be amidst a perfect artistic expression of nature, yet not feel the aliveness that I was accustomed to?

Lizard Head Pass is a year-round playground. In the winter it is ideal for cross-country skiing, snowshoeing and snowmobiling. During the remainder of the year, with its prominent peaks, green plateaus and abundant wildlife, it is a vast playground for hiking, camping, climbing and adventuring. With all these possibilities for fun, it occurred to me that it doesn't matter where we are physically. What matters is where we are emotionally. If we don't have our health or we're not happy on the inside, it doesn't matter how big or beautiful the playground really is. I hopped back into my truck, aware of the small emotional storm brewing inside me. Ordinarily, I would be thrilled to be on Lizard Head Pass. Yet this time I wasn't feeling my normal connection to one of my favorite play areas in the San Juans.

I slowly reentered the highway and continued on toward Rico, a onetime mining town whose history seemed to parallel my own patterns. Rico started out as a small mining town in 1866 and grew explosively as the gold rush boomed throughout southwestern Colorado. By 1900, seven years after the boom went bust, the population had dwindled from 5,000 to barely 800. It has never fully recovered. Driving through town, I felt as though I could relate to the emotions of the many miners who gave up on their dreams and left town. My boom days felt like they were behind me, and I was looking for a new way to live and enjoy my life. It was my hope that this journey to Chaco Canyon would help me rediscover the vein of gold in my heart and mind.

Rico is a typical three-blink mountain town. You can drive from one side of the town to the other with three blinks of your eyes. On my third blink I had driven past all the historical buildings, and was on my way to Dolores and Durango.

Dolores is a brief stop. Unlike Rico, which is a mining town, Dolores is in the heart of Mesa Verde Country, and was originally established as a train station supporting the Rio Grande Southern Railway. It is now a passageway to Durango, Cortez and Telluride, and known for its hunting, biking, fly fishing, boating, hiking and chuck wagon dinners. I enjoy the simplicity of Dolores, but my real connection to the town is knowing that my high school friend Taz Vass owns the local grocery store. Every time I drive through town, I am reminded of fun childhood memories.

Arriving in Durango represents my halfway mark to Chaco Canyon. This historical mountain town holds a special place in my heart. It reminds me of some of my happiest childhood memories. When I was a kid, I fell in love with steam- and coal-driven railroads. I still have my Marklin train set from my early childhood days. Durango is a train lover's dream. It is the home to the historical coal-burning, steam-powered, narrow-gauge Denver and Rio Grande Railroad. Every time I enter Durango, and smell the smoke from the burning coal, it takes me back to my childhood. Originally built to transport gold and silver ore, the train is now Durango's main attraction, touring visitors year-round through the breathtaking San Juan Mountains. One of my favorite memories of Durango is a winter ride on the train with my best friend, Michael Cordova.

Between Durango's mining history and the joy of my childhood memories, Durango offered me a beautiful blend of the pioneering spirit and the sweet taste of my own youthful innocence and enthusiasm.

As I drove out of town, and said goodbye to the railroad, I couldn't help but be aware of the common thread shared by Telluride, Rico, Durango and Dolores. They were all established by people with a pioneering spirit, people who saw the unseen and believed in possibilities. They had positive expectations for the future and were willing to take risks in order to progress toward their dreams. When they looked at mountains, they didn't just see just the surface, with its trees, rocks and dirt. They saw possibilities. They knew that the only way in life to find or create anything of value was to look past appearances...to look past obstacles...to keep their eyes set on their goals.

Even though I wasn't pioneering new territory on this journey, I was pioneering my own spirit, creating the emotional space to look deep into my own life. As I left Durango, the mountain landscape flattened into desert, and my reflections upon the accomplishments of those early pioneers gave me plenty of perspective for looking at my own life.

I drove the next eighty miles at a calm speed, enjoying my music while noticing the change in landscape. Two hours later, I arrived at the Nageezi entrance to Chaco Canyon. I pulled off the road to take a picture of the entrance sign, stretch my body, and breathe in the fresh, warm, desert air. Tucked away at the side of the road, about thirty feet from the entrance and two feet off the ground, was another sign that was strangled with sage and barely readable.

ROUGH ROAD.

MAY BE IMPASSABLE.

TRAVEL AT YOUR OWN RISK!

A warning sign is just that: a warning. But it's not an absolute. It's a warning that something may happen. As I read the sign, I remember thinking, "Wouldn't it be cool if life gave us warning signs when we're going in the wrong direction or making bad choices?" Then I reflected and realized that it does, but we're not always listening or paying attention.

After a few minutes of teetering around the entrance, I hopped back into my Tacoma and entered the twenty-one miles of unmaintained dirt road the signs had warned me about. I created my own meditative desert atmosphere by playing Richard Warner's Quiet Heart CD. Quiet Heart is peaceful bamboo flute music for wizards. It stills the mind and opens the heart.

The road was a bit of a challenge. It was slow and dusty and subject to flash floods, herds of sheep and high winds — everything I could want in a mystical adventure into the past. The high-desert landscape that surrounded me was sparsely painted with cactus, sagebrush, pinion and juniper, and was far more breathtaking than I could have imagined. About five miles into the drive, I stopped again to take in the stark beauty of the terrain. The air was warm, dry, and filled with the aromatic bouquet of fresh sage.

Though the land is calm and still, an abundance of wildlife quietly blends into the background of the arid terrain. Coyotes, mule deers, elk, bobcats, badgers, foxes, skunks, prairie dogs, bats, roadrunners, hawks, owls, vultures, ravens, hummingbirds, rattlesnakes and lizards are the faces and souls of the desert. As I gazed into the vastness of the desert, I imagined millions of hidden eyes staring back at me.

When I finally reached the main entrance, I felt a huge rush of excitement as I caught my first glimpse of the ancient ruins. I stopped at the visitor center to get a map and historical guide of the area so that I could learn the basic history of Chaco Canyon and the ancient Anasazi. After a warm and friendly discussion with the park rangers, I sat down outside to begin my mental tour of the history of a beautiful and ancient people. What I discovered gave me a deeper glimpse into why this area is so well-known for having sacred value.

Even though I came here for spiritual retreat, I had a feeling that learning about the lifestyle of this culture would inspire me to look at my own life differently.

THREE

Ancient Ruins

A day is Eternity's seed, and we are its Gardeners.

~ Erika Harris

THE HISTORY OF CHACO CANYON goes back thousands of years to when it was one of the main roaming grounds for the nomadic people of the Southwest. The Basket Makers were the first to appear in the Southwest and existed as an evolving culture between approximately 1200 BC and 750 AD. They gained their name because they hand-crafted beautiful, finely woven, flexible and seamless baskets, trays and bowls using fibers from desert plants.

The early Basket Makers were primarily hunters who camped in the open or lived in caves. In about 700 AD, the Basket Makers began settling in the canyon and constructing small one-story masonry pueblos. A century later, the more modern Basket Makers, known as the Anasazi, began building permanent structures throughout the canyon. The structures were most often oriented in the solar, lunar, and cardinal directions, and included astronomical markers and other features for communication and ceremony. In the two hundred years that followed, more than four hundred Anasazi sites were constructed within sixty miles of the present-day cultural center.

The Anasazi were deeply immersed in the path of their spiritual beliefs. Their roads, dwellings and kivas (ceremonial rooms) were the vehicles through which they expressed their devotion on a daily basis. Every detail of their design had significance. The placement of the structures in proximity to each other, and in relation to the roads and stars, played a critical role in how they lived their lives. The many petroglyphs of the solar and lunar cycles found on the surrounding cliffs and throughout the structure emphasize the important role astronomy played in their lives.

The Anasazi lived their life on their feet. They did not have wheels or beasts of burden, yet they built more than two hundred miles of connecting roads with brilliant efficiency, serving a population of some five thousand people. At a time when most Europeans were living in thatched huts, the Anasazi were developing multistory structures with hundreds of rooms. Within a hundred years of the expansion of Chaco Canyon, the Anasazi began to abandon their pueblos. By 1200 AD Chaco had been completely vacated.

In just a few hundred years, an organized culture with thousands of years of prehistory rose and fell. This dramatic history is reduced to a nine-mile loop that takes you along the major sites of this ancient culture. The two most historically significant sites are Pueblo Bonito and Chetro Ketl.

I entered the loop with quiet enthusiasm. These are not just ancient ruins. This is a culture whose entire lifestyle was based on their spiritual beliefs. Entering the ruins demanded the highest level of respect for an ancient people and a notable time in history.

My first stop was at Chetro Ketl, Chaco's second-largest structure. Covering more than three acres, it has the largest surface area of any of the structures, yet has only four or five hundred rooms, twelve kivas and a single great kiva. As I walked around the remains, I couldn't help but feel the powerful hand of time. Everything has its own lifetime, and we can have many lifetimes within one life. Each of these kivas represents a lifetime of traditions, and a place of transformation and growth. How wonderful it would be, I thought, if a ceremony would begin right now, offering me an opportunity to join in and cleanse my spirit and clear my heart and mind.

I closed my eyes and imagined myself standing amidst hundreds of Anasazi, singing, chanting and dancing to the beat of drums. I imagined that we had just returned from a hunt using wood clubs, hunting sticks and spears. I saw us clothed in garments of fur and feathers, our sandals made of woven yucca strips, and our bodies adorned with beads and pendants carved from stones, bones and shells. While we were out hunting, the women would have been gathering amaranth, sunflower seeds, pinion nuts and mustard seeds, all of which would be used to create cooking flour. Our meals would be prepared by dropping red-hot stones into waterproof cooking baskets, and mixing in the flour and liquid. The meal would be served after our evening of ceremony and ritual cleansing. I imagined entering the ceremonial kiva, surrounded by dozens of other Anasazi, and moving in a clockwise direction until I faced the direction of the full moon. The heat from the volcanic rocks would force my body into a heat-induced hallucination. The sound of beating drums and the echoes of chanting would fill my mind until I had a vision of my own body covered in blood from the sacrifice of my fears. A loud scream from deep in my imaginings jolted me back into the present. I opened my eyes, drenched in a cold sweat, awed by a power I hadn't anticipated.

Had that vision been a true journey into the past, a creative journey through my imagination, or a premonition?

I moved next to Pueblo Bonito, the largest structure at Chaco Canyon and, by far, the most magnificent. Located on nearly two acres in the center of Chaco Canyon, it was occupied between 850 AD and 1250 AD. It originally rose four to five stories high, with upwards of eight hundred rooms, thirty-two kivas and three larger "great" kivas.

As I walked around Pueblo Bonito, I allowed my imagination to take me back to the time when this was an active community. I stood next to one of the great kivas and imagined that in the not too distant past, someone else had stood in the very same spot, breathing the same desert air, preparing to enter the kiva for spiritual ceremony. I marveled at how real all this had been to them. Now, they don't even exist as a memory, and the kiva is a relic of times past. I thought about my own life. When I die, will I leave anything behind as beautiful as this kiva? Or will my life become a forgotten memory? Intuitively, I knew the answer. It would be up to me.

Even though I had come to Chaco Canyon to find rest and relaxation, the unspoken lessons from these ruins threw my mind into an internal dialogue of curiosity. I felt like a kid. It was one thing to just look at the ruins and observe their powerful innocence. It was another to actually use my imagination and immerse myself in their culture. One single artifact on the ground, a petroglyph on the rock walls or a window in any of the pueblos was enough to immerse me in a visionary experience.

Had it not been for the intense dry desert heat, I could have explored all day without rest. Yet after about two hours, I was ready to take a break and cool off in the air-conditioning of my truck. I returned to the Casa Rinconda parking area and crossed paths with a woman who was visiting from Santa Fe. She asked if I had seen the incredible artifacts on the Pueblo Alto trail. I hadn't. She insisted that if I had the time, it would be worth the visit and would only take a few hours. With so much still weighing on my mind and plenty of time, I saw no harm in following her suggestion. After cooling off, munching on some organic grapes and strawberries and rehydrating with pure Colorado mountain water, I drove over to the parking area for the Pueblo Alto Loop, parked my truck, filled my backpack with snacks, walked to the trailhead, registered my name and license plate in the permit box, and began the hike west along an old road that leads to the trailhead of the Pueblo Alto Loop.

The Pueblo Alto Loop rises from the floor of Chaco Canyon to the top of a large plateau. From the trailhead, I hiked upwards over car-sized rubble until I reached the mouth of a four-foot-wide crack canyon. I entered the narrow corridor using natural handholds in the rock to guide my balance and propel myself upward. The corridor was sheltered from the sun, and a cool breeze filled the air. I paid close attention to the variations in the texture of the stone, and even noticed ancient seashells embedded into a small area of the rock wall.

Once I reached the top of the hundred-foot ascent, the corridor widened and I emerged onto the plateau overlooking Chaco Canyon. The magical panoramic views took my breath away. The spectacular collage of desert flora, rock formations, fossils, petroglyphs and ancient ruins all merged to open a gateway for imagination and introspection.

There's a lot more going on at Chaco than meets the eye. For some, it is simply a beautiful place of historical significance offering a stunning window into the past. For the more inquisitive mind, it's a testimony to the various possibilities for the future of humanity.

As I continued on with my hike, taking in the scenery and enjoying the many artifacts, I began to explore a whole different level of questions...

What is humanity doing to itself at this point in time? The Anasazi lived off the land and were relatively harmless toward nature. Yet they vanished with no historical explanation. Today, we are manipulating the entire ecosystem by poisoning the earth with chemicals, destroying our oceans, rivers and rain forests, polluting our air, and eliminating indigenous tribes. We are genetically modifying our food, processing it, filling it with artificial chemicals, flavors, preservatives and sweeteners...essentially turning it into poison. Yet we call it food just because it looks pretty and tastes yummy.

What is going on with humanity that we are so self-destructive? Why do we poison our own air, water and food? Why are we fighting so much? Why are we killing each other and destroying our planet with such reckless abandon and rabid ambivalence? Why are so many people okay with this?

Most of the world acts as if we are separate from nature, as if we can do whatever we want to our planet without any consequence. People are afraid of HIV, cancer, diabetes, swine flu and any of a number of diseases. Yet at the same time, our eating habits and social and cultural behaviors are entirely self-destructive and destructive to the planet. People complain about oil spills, deforestation and other disasters. Yet, on a daily basis, we utilize endless amounts of toxic cleaning products and toxic personal-care products, all of which enter our body, our air, our water, and our food chain.

The real virus killing us is the "virus" of ignorance, laziness and arrogance, which is far more destructive than any environmental disaster, biological virus or disease will ever pretend to be.

- ❖ Our ignorance of who we truly are and what we are capable of, as individuals and collectively as humanity.
- ❖ Our lazy attitude toward our personal power and genetic potential.
- ❖ Our arrogance that we believe we can bomb one part of the planet and not have it affect the entire planet.
- ❖ Our arrogance that we believe there is no relationship between what we think and eat, and the overall quality of our physical, mental and emotional health.
- ❖ Our arrogance that we believe it's okay, as individuals or collectively as humanity, to treat people, ourselves and the earth the way we do.

Unfortunately, there is no vaccine for this virus. But there is a remedy: awareness...awareness of the truth of who we are and what we are capable of, individually and collectively. The challenge is, how do we expand awareness? How do we contribute to a global shift in consciousness that would move humanity into a more sustainable direction?

These are important questions to me. I have been asking them most of my life. Yet on this hike, the unspoken message delivered through the ruins was loud and clear: The disappearance of an entire culture and civilization is not a very promising or encouraging outcome. Yet it is a powerful warning if we don't wake up and do something to change.

Continuing on with my hike, with the pace of my thoughts accelerating, I stopped at the Pueblo Bonito overlook. It was the perfect place to take a break, stretch my body and quiet my mind. I was awestruck by what I saw. If Chaco Canyon is a window into the past, then standing on the Pueblo Bonito overlook was like looking through a skylight from above and seeing the past as one magnificent mosaic of nature and time. It was here on the Pueblo Bonito overlook that I found the desert contrast I had imagined. Emptiness and fullness could be seen and felt with my eyes and my emotions. The entire landscape was carved and sculpted with the power of heat and cold, wind and sunshine, dryness and moisture. Empty space was filled with sprinklings of organic life, and desert flowers were smiling amidst the vastness of arid terrain. It was here that everything made sense. When we look at life from above, the whole picture comes into focus.

Looking down on Pueblo Bonito stretches the mind to its outer limits. These are not just ruins of an ancient culture. They are an historical storybook representing thousands of years of social transformation. The Anasazi were crafters of the highest caliber. They felt with their heart, created with their mind and crafted with their hands. It's a fascinating mental exercise trying to visualize and comprehend the entire cycle from discovery to abandonment to now. Yet right there in front of me was an open tombstone of an ancient culture.

My eyes filled with tears as I reflected on the parallels between the demise of the Anasazi and our current state of world affairs. My peaceful journey turned into deep inquiry into the purpose of my own life. Looking over the cliff toward Pueblo Bonito, I reviewed my core questions.

- ❖ What can I do with my life that will be meaningful and fulfilling?
- ❖ How can I create a true sense of purpose and passion?
- ❖ How do I stop looking back upon the difficult times in my life with fear, and start looking forward with courage and wisdom?
- ❖ How can I let go of the old thoughts and beliefs that are holding me back from realizing my potential, and how do I replace them with new, empowering beliefs?

Some people say that life is a gift. Yet a gift is never received until it is opened. What, I wondered as I stood there, am I supposed to do with this gift? How do I open it? Was life a gift to the Anasazi? But look what happened to them. What can I do with my gift? Can I truly make a positive difference in this world? Will anyone want to hear what I have to say, or am I just another peace-lover touring the universe?

I love people, I love life, and I want to make a positive difference in the world. Like everyone, I have made my fair share of mistakes; some big, some small. Yet they have all been my greatest lessons. And my "enemies" have been my greatest teachers. Somehow, standing high above that desert expanse, I wanted to take the experiences of my life, of my travels around the world, and use them to create something meaningful and rewarding for myself and all of humanity.

My thoughts about life were quickly being overpowered by the afternoon heat. I gathered my CamelBak and continued on with my quest. The trail was marked with rock cairns, which made it easy to stay on course. I grabbed my iPod from my CamelBak and started listening to Carlos Nakai, one of my favorite Native American artists. I was now about one mile into my hike and I crossed paths with a group of people from Arizona who were on their way down. They gave me some tips about the trail and reassured me that I was going in the right direction.

The trail started flattening out and I was finally able to walk at a calm pace and enjoy the silence of the desert. I started to notice the lizards, desert flora, cacti, insects and small petroglyphs that could be missed by a busy, preoccupied mind. The lizards were so much fun to watch. What an interesting life they live! They blend perfectly into the desert landscape and are only noticeable when they move. They stand perfectly still until they are approached and then once noticed, they dart across the land with a huge burst of lightning-speed energy. They can walk up walls, walk upside down, and stick to the surface in any direction. More incredibly, they are female-only and never have the experience of pursuing a hot, sexy young male lizard to be their mate. One lizard challenged me to a staring contest. But once I moved my hand to scratch an itch on my nose, she disappeared in the blink of an eye.

Continuing on, I was beginning to become aware of the intensity of the heat. I looked down and I realized that I had virtually no shadow, which meant the sun was directly above me. For my own safety, I decided to move toward a cooler part of the trail to minimize my heat exposure. The flat trail turned into a soft sand-like path that wound along a tall rock formation. Even though the sun was still directly above me, it was cooler walking on the sand than directly on the rock. The path turned into a bit of a desert oasis. On my left were sagebrush and cactus, mingled with dry forests of juniper and piñon. In the sand you could see dried up trails of where water drained after a rainstorm. Even though my feet were cooler, I began experiencing two types of heat. The sun was beating down directly onto my head, and the radiant heat from the rock wall on my right was penetrating my body. My bandana was protecting my head. Yet I was still beginning to feel like a bag of microwave popcorn getting ready to pop.

Desert heat is different than mountain heat. In the desert, much of your sweat evaporates off your body, without you ever seeing it or feeling it. So the potential for overheating or heat stroke is much higher than in the mountains. I was starting to sense this possibility, so I shifted closer to the nearby rock wall to walk along a more shaded part of the trail.

Within five minutes of this cooler path, I had a collision with destiny and my life was forever changed.

FOUR

Collision With Destiny

The path is clear, the way is certain. In the crossing, my eyes must join, my heart must sing and my ears must hear. The training is over. It is now or never. And in the choosing, I become the destiny and image of my choices.
  ~ David Lloyd Strauss

I STARTED MY DAY in peaceful solitude looking for answers to questions about my life. My day started out beautifully. It was everything I wanted. Chaco Canyon was the perfect setting for introspection and quietness of heart and mind, until I chose to walk closer to the wall. In one moment, I was cooling down from the arid heat while enjoying a beautiful walk in the desert. The next thing I knew, I was lying on the ground and my head and body were covered in blood.

At that moment, at around 12:30 in the afternoon, I was hit on the head by a falling rock, was knocked unconscious and later awakened to discover that I was alone on the desert plateau with no one in the vicinity to rescue me. My scalp was split open, I was lightheaded and dizzy, and my vision was blurring.

When I look back now, I vaguely remember the moment the rock landed on my head. As soon as it hit, I put my hand on my head, felt a hole and felt the warmth of my own blood pouring onto my face and body. My adrenaline shot through the roof, I screamed Noooooooooooooo! and slowly collapsed to the ground. As I was collapsing, I truly thought that my life was ending. I crossed that magical bridge that leads away from the worrisome world of humanity and entered into the timeless moment that everyone fears. I don't know how long I was out, but when I awakened, I found myself far out on the trail and hidden from immediate sight. My hike shifted from sightseeing and daydreaming to seeking out my own self-rescue.

As I opened my eyes, my head was spinning out of control and I was completely disoriented. I had no idea where I was or what had just happened to me. I felt the warmth of the sun on my body, yet I was shivering as if I was lying in a bathtub full of ice. My eyes fell shut again.

Is this a dream? Have I just died? Is this death?
What is that pain I'm feeling on the top of my head?
Why does my head feel so warm and wet?
"Hello? Hello?"

A voice kept telling me to wake up, to get up. I opened my eyes again and stared ahead. My eyes slowly focused on the rock wall next to me.

Rock wall? Sand...? Am I in the desert? Holy shit! What just happened?

After an inner silence that seemed to last for hours, I heard the screams of a bird. I looked up and saw a hawk circling high above me. My godfather goes by the name Hawkwind.

What was the last conversation I had with him? I told him I was going to Chaco Canyon. Holy shit! Am I in Chaco Canyon? Why am I on the ground? Did I fall asleep? Did I get heatstroke?

23

The pain on my head grew stronger and more intense. I glanced down toward my body and froze emotionally as I discovered that I was covered with blood. It was then that I suspected that I had a head injury.

Do I move or don't I? What if I also have a neck and spinal injury? I have to examine my head. Can I move my arms without moving my neck or back?

I had no idea what the overall condition of my body was. I just knew that blood and dizziness are signs of trouble. Although I've had my share of sports injuries, they were all to my limbs. Broken bones, sprains and lacerations have brought plenty of pain into my life, but a head injury was a new experience.

How was I to rescue myself if I couldn't think or see clearly? Cell phones don't work in Chaco Canyon, so this was one of those moments when all I had to rely on were the resources of nature, the contents of my daypack, my own thoughts, and time. Once I'd gathered my thoughts, I started to "Google" every part of my brain, searching for answers of what to do. I realized that I had two choices. I could remain still and hope for someone to find and rescue me, or I could risk self-rescue. This was an agonizing choice because each was potentially harmful...or fatal. If I waited, there was the possibility that no one would find me. If I chose self-rescue, there was the possibility of further harm.

For the first time in my life, I truly understood the depth to which our choices affect our lives. Every choice we make in life has its own set of possibilities and outcomes. Our decisions — our choices — are defining moments in the overall direction of our life. It doesn't matter what happens to us in life. What matters is the choice we make as a result of our experiences. In this situation, all choices fell upon the current condition of my body, which was a huge unknown.

Before I made any decisions, the only thing I could do was draw upon my first-responder training, and do a physical self-assessment to determine whether I had broken bones in my back, neck or elsewhere. As I had taken a rock to my head, the potential for neck or spine injury was very high. Hope for the best, prepare for the worst.

I will never forget the excruciating moment when I delicately moved my right arm from my side and raised it up toward my head. The sun was beating down on me like a steak in a broiler. My eyes were caked and burning from the salt of my sweat and blood. I was dizzy, slightly deranged and alone. I was truly terrified, because if I had seriously hurt my neck or back, the slightest move could sever my spine and leave me paralyzed. I gingerly raised my hand and moved my fingers along the sore area of my scalp. Suddenly, my fingers slipped into the hole in my scalp and I realized that I had an open head injury. Yet I was still alive. My adrenaline shot through the roof and I started becoming more alert. The wetness I was feeling was my own blood.

I knew I had to put direct pressure on my open wound. But I also had to feel my neck and spine for bruising, swelling or displaced bones. I did not feel comfortable using both arms until I was sure that my neck and spine weren't injured. Too much movement was potentially disastrous. So I chose to allow my head to continue to bleed while I examined my neck and spine. My neck was definitely sore. This could have been either reactive pain from my neck muscles responding to the rock and my fall, or referral pain from a deeper vertebrae injury. I assessed my neck one more time by pressing my fingers a bit harder against my vertebrae. I didn't feel any pain in my bones, so I took a leap of faith and assumed that my neck had not been injured. Now, I had to control the bleeding from my head. With an odd blend of panic and humor, I realized that my only two choices were a tourniquet or direct pressure. I moved my fingers along my head to find the hole and began pressing the palm of my hand directly onto the wound.

Next, I needed to assess my mid- and lower back for damage. I did this with my other hand and arm. It was a bit trickier because it meant twisting my body a bit more in order to maneuver my hand along my spine. This was anything but graceful. With each movement of my body, I plunged into fear and massive uncertainty. My self-assessment would either rescue me or destroy me.

What a strange turn in events. Only a short while earlier, I'd been having a playful staring contest with a lizard and enjoying a beautiful day of reflection. The only reason I was on this trail was because I'd chosen to follow the suggestion of a stranger in the parking lot. Now, I was bathed in my own blood, making life-altering decisions.

After completing my full spinal assessment, I felt cautiously confident that my neck and spine were stable. At that point, I decided that if I was to live to see the end of the day, I would have to rescue myself. With my right hand on my head, I stood up cautiously. Not cautiously enough. A huge head rush dropped me back onto the ground. Standing up was not going to be as easy as I'd thought.

With my right hand pressed into my wound, I grabbed my CamelBak with my left hand, rehydrated myself and stood up again, this time even more carefully. I leaned up against the rock wall to hold my balance and to become more clear about where I was and where I needed to go. Although I didn't remember the trail or the direction that I came from, I noticed two sets of cairns marking a trail along the rocky path. I moved very slowly toward the cairns until I came upon a sandy part of the trail. Embedded in the sand was a set of footprints pointing in the direction from which I had just walked. They were my footprints. I felt an incredible sense of relief. Those footprints saved my life. They became, my Footsteps After The Fall.

I was still in unknown territory. Though I knew I was moving in the right direction, I was lightheaded and dizzy and my head was still bleeding. On top of that, the heat was pounding on my head, intensifying an already pounding headache. My whole body ached. Even my groin was screaming from the apparent stress on my double hernia. The emotional pain was even more intense. There wasn't another person in sight.

Every step I took was cautious, yet deliberate. My main objective was to get myself into an area with maximum visibility so that I could be found by other hikers. I knew I had to move quickly. But I also had to be careful to pace myself: I didn't want to increase blood-flow to my head, and I didn't want to cause any more tearing in my hernia.

I knew one thing for certain: Our emotional response to any situation has a huge impact on the outcome of that situation. I could not afford any negative thoughts or feelings of hopelessness. If I was to make it out of there, I had to be more than positive and hopeful. I had to take complete control of my emotions and tap into my deepest reservoir of strength and courage. Even though I was still bleeding from my head and had all the symptoms of a severe concussion, I had to do the opposite of what seemed logical: I had to connect with the positive emotions of believing that I was healed and of being grateful for the healing. By doing this, I would have the best chance of positively impacting my healing and rescue.

I knew what I needed to do emotionally. Yet there were other forces at play. With each step, I danced with every emotion you can imagine: fear, anger, resentment, laughter, gratitude, hope, uncertainty, courage, blame, abandonment, and acceptance. I did my best to keep it together, yet the experience of believing my life had ended and then waking up with a bloody concussion opened an emotional valve in my heart that was releasing a lifetime of emotion. There was no way of preventing this emotional flood from taking its natural course. The rivers of my heart were flooded with emotions, and the river was running freely.

The rock on my head was far more than an unexpected injury. The lid on my emotional jar of life had been screwed on so tightly that it took a rock to crack it open. The resulting hole in my head was the release valve that would begin to free emotional roadblocks that had been building up since I was twelve...feelings of loneliness, rejection and abandonment...fears of loss of love and betrayal. These feelings were rooted in the childhood experience of my mom's illness and of her death when I was fifteen. In the years since, those emotions had grown roots and buried themselves deep in my heart.

Clearly, this was not an ideal time to analyze my life. But when you're in survival mode, covered with blood and pumped with adrenaline, many strange things play out in your mind.

My teary outbursts were tiresome. Yet each release of tears also released decades-old emotional burdens, burdens I had borne so deeply that I hadn't even realized I was carrying them. I began feeling lighter and lighter. Joy and gratitude started washing over me. I somehow realized that my injury had been a gift, a message that I was now ready to let go of old, self-limiting ideas of who I was. It was time for me to find a new, empowering reason to make sense of my life and to live and love at a much deeper and meaningful level than I had ever lived before.

Feeling the lightness of emotional release, with each step I kept repeating out loud…

I am so happy and grateful now that I am healed!
God's timing is perfect!
I am surrounded by angels.

I kept repeating this over and over, aloud so that I could hear myself affirming my own thoughts and beliefs. I said it emphatically, with pure emotion and belief. With my head covered with sweat and blood, I really had no choice but to believe this, because any other belief would have been self-destructive.

As I staggered down the trail, doing my best to retain clarity over my emotions, I was clearly surviving on adrenaline. There was enough heat to roast a turkey, I was overheated and dehydrated, and my vision was wavering between focused and merry-go-round spin. I had rolled the dice when I chose to rescue myself, and now I was feeling the impact of that choice.

The Pueblo Alto Loop is very popular. I had every reason to believe that there would be other people along the trail. My entire plan had been built around making it to an open area where others could find me and rescue me. With each bend of the path, I expected another hiker to materialize and come to my rescue. Yet I had still not seen a single soul, not even a small body in the distance. The uncertainty of being rescued was testing my courage. If I wasn't going to be found on this trail, my next best chance was to make it to the Pueblo Bonito overlook, which is the most popular part of the trail.

To complicate my already difficult situation, both of my hands and arms were beginning to tingle, and I was losing sensation in my fingers. As the numbness increased, I grew increasingly nervous and paused in the heat to further assess my body. I had to quickly determine the cause of this loss in sensation and act accordingly. It could either be the result of blood loss, a head or spinal injury, pinched nerves in my shoulders from the straps of my CamelBak, or any combination of these. I was still able to move at a careful and safe pace and had enough balance to stand. I took another leap of faith and assumed that it was the straps. But that involved another uncomfortable decision, because it would take two hands to loosen my CamelBak. Would it be better to remove my right hand from my wound to adjust the straps, but risk additional blood-loss? Or should I continue to suffer the slow loss of sensation in my arms and hands? There really was no choice. I would soon need full use of my left hand for the final part of the climb through the crack canyon. For right now, I needed the feeling sensation in my hand to ensure that I was keeping pressure on my wound.

As I stood on a huge rock formation, heat radiating from the rock into my feet and body, both hands and arms tingling, I removed my hand from my wound, quickly unlocked my waist strap, loosened the tension on both my shoulder straps and then immediately returned to pressure to my wound. My head was again covered with fresh blood, yet the tingling had subsided and sensation quickly returned to my arms and hands.

Taking a deep breath, and feeling a huge sigh of relief, I returned to my positive affirmations and resumed my descent. About twenty minutes later, when I reached the halfway mark, I was feeling even more overheated, dehydrated and lightheaded. I was also having a hard time seeing because the blood covering my face and eyelids was beginning to dry and crust over like thickly caked mud. I desperately needed to rinse my face with water so that I could again see clearly. As before, this would require me to take my hand off my wound so that I could hold my CamelBak over my head, while using my other hand to open the pinch-valve. Again, I had no choice. After gulping down some water, I removed my hand from my wound, took the CamelBak off my back, held it over my head with my right hand, grabbed the supply hose with my left hand, opened the valve with my fingers, and began a rapid cleaning of my face and eyes. I held my face up so that the blood would drip down the back of my head instead of back into my eyes.

As quickly as I could, I put the CamelBak back on, returned pressure to my wound, drank some more water, assessed my balance and vision, and continued my descent. Every step seemed like an eternity, and there was still no one in sight. As I approached the overlook, I was growing more and more tired, yet I was still juiced on adrenaline. The reality that this entire event would require self-rescue was becoming more and more apparent.

With hopeful anticipation, I finally made it to the overlook. I felt as if my soul had been ripped from my body. There was no one in sight. My plan had failed. I stood there for a timeless moment, emotionally frozen. The situation was bleak. I surrendered to my pain and my fears. I let out a primal scream and collapsed to the ground in total exhaustion. My face, head and neck were burnt, and my courage began melting away with the heat of the sun. My heart and head throbbed like a beating drum. I was panting like a thirsty dog, and my head, face and body were encrusted with sweat and blood. I burst into tears as I questioned my destiny. Would I be found? Did I have the energy to continue? I closed my eyes in quiet desperation, and experienced the longest moment of my life. I watched my entire life in a fast-forward replay and tried to make sense of who I was and what had brought me to this moment.

How was this possible? Where had I gone wrong? Throughout my life there have been many times when I have lived on the edge in extreme sports such as skydiving, rock- or ice-climbing, bungee-jumping, cliff-jumping, extreme skiing and mountaineering, any of which easily could have killed me. Yet none had. In 1996, for example, I climbed to the 23,000-foot summit of Aconcagua, Argentina, the tallest mountain in the western and southern hemispheres, in extreme, desolate winter conditions, with temperatures approaching minus 100 degrees Fahrenheit. Yet I came out of it out with nothing but magical memories. But here I was, on a beautiful, sunny, dry, carefree day, alone on a popular day-hike trail, having been hit on the head by a falling rock.

The odds this day had been in my favor, not against me. Not only am I a safe and cautious outdoor-adventure athlete, nothing about this hike could have signaled falling rocks as an imminent danger. It was feeling as though this entire day had been predetermined. I had hiked up here at the suggestion of a woman from Arizona. My choice to do so had led me to a trail where a rock was teetering on collapse, seemingly waiting for me to show up so that it could give me a near-death experience. But why? Why had this happened? Of all the possibilities for this day, why a rock on my head? Why had I woken up with such a strong determination to reorient my mind and rescue myself? Why had I found my own footsteps leading me back onto the main trail?

My life was feeling like a board game without a clear set of rules. Instead, the rules were being made as I went along. Every time I rolled the dice, I would take a few steps forward and something would be there to both challenge me and help me move forward. Everything seemed like it was laid out in advance, and I only needed to discover the clues that would bring me home. I never knew if something would be an obstacle or a clue until I took the next step. Yet even with all of the clues I uncovered, I had arrived at a point of total exhaustion. Being clueless was not an option. I had to figure out my next move or I would die. What was my next clue?

It felt like I had been laying there for years. Nothing seemed real any more, not even the moment. I went deep inside my heart and dug for the energy and courage to continue. It was in that timeless moment, with my head spinning and my eyes pouring out tears of helplessness, that I remembered words of wisdom my stepfather had shared with me during my mother's illness:

Don't ever think your problems are any better or any worse than anyone else's. They're just yours. When you learn to embrace your problems and see them as teachers in disguise, you will be able to handle any difficulty you face.

These words gave me the courage to deal with my mother's illness and death. Now, thirty years later, they are again saving my life. Today is not going to be my last day on this planet. This is not going to be my day of death. Not here, not now. Feeling the depth of my stepfather's words, I realized that I couldn't wait for anyone to rescue me. There was too much at stake. My only option was self-rescue. I had to take full responsibility for my life. I had to find the inner strength to do it. And I had to do it now!

I did the only thing I could do: listen. I listened to my thoughts and listened to my heart, and it was there that I found the next clue. I am still alive in this moment in time because I made a decision to rescue myself. And through my self-rescue, the love that had always been in my heart was fully exposed through the release of my tears.

All the love and courage I was ever looking for was always within my very own heart. Yet it was deeply buried behind the walls of emotional pain. Reflecting upon these thoughts, I knew I had it in me to carry on. Everything I needed was within me. Everything we ever need is always within us, always within our own hearts.

With the shallow of my breath, I whispered a prayer.

Great Spirit of Light and Love. Thank you for the life that I have been given. I surrender who I am and what I am to the forces of nature and the power of love. Breathe through me the breath that will take me home. Thank you Spirit. Thank you Angels.

In that moment of complete surrender, I felt a huge knot in my belly explode, and all the energy that was going into tears moved its way into my breath. I started breathing more heavily, almost to the point of hyperventilating. I felt as though I was being resuscitated by an unseen force, as if something had entered my body and was breathing through me, as me. With these breaths, I tapped into an inner strength of unknown magnitude that gave me the resilience to continue on. I drank my last sips of water, and squeezed out a few drops to rinse my face and clear my eyes.

With my heart beating like the drum roll before a daring acrobatic act, I cautiously raised myself off the ground, wiped the sweat and blood off my sunglasses and began moving forward. With each step, under the softness of my breath, I said…

Thank You – Thank You – Thank You
Thank you for the breath.
Thank you for the healing.
Thank you for taking me home.

My steps and breath were trancelike. I felt like I was sleepwalking. Was I? Was this really happening? I couldn't tell the difference between the outside world and my inside world. Everything felt like a virtual movie, and the plot kept changing. It was real. I was living on borrowed time. Who was I borrowing it from? Myself? Angels? Earth energy?

I had another 1.6 miles to go. It might as well have been one hundred miles. All my sense of time and distance had collapsed. It was the most powerful place I had ever been in. I was living in the moment. Not the past or the future, but the moment. I was alive and walking because I wanted to be. I had chosen life and, through that choice, my deepest reservoirs of strength and courage opened up and carried me forward.

The final part of the trail was treacherous. At the beginning of the hike, I'd had to climb one hundred feet up a crack canyon. Now I had to climb down that same canyon with a concussion, dehydration, blood loss, one arm and an irritated double hernia. The trail was an obstacle course of large, unstable boulders, small rocks and a narrow path. I had to keep pressure on my wound, so I began the climb down relying on my left hand and what little mental balance I had available. I was grossly overheated and noticeably dizzy. After my first few steps into the crack canyon, I lost my footing, slipped and fell forward. By some miracle, I caught myself with my left hand by grabbing onto a part of the rock wall, preventing what could have easily been a tragic ending to my self-rescue. After catching my breath and balance, I began a slower descent. With each step I affirmed to myself, "I made it down safely. I made it down safely."

I finally made it to the trailhead where I found another hiker. I told him my name and briefly described what had happened. He quickly gave me sips of water, led me to my truck and drove me to the Ranger Station, where I was rehydrated, offered a place to cool down and given my initial first aid. The ranger told me that the nearest hospital was eighty miles away, and that it would take up to two hours for an ambulance to arrive. This meant that it would be at least four hours before I could get medical treatment.

Even though I was now safely with the ranger, I was amped on adrenaline and connected to a profound source of inner courage, strength and energy. When I was at the Pueblo Bonito overlook, I had realized that there was too much at risk for me to wait for anyone to rescue me. I had to take total responsibility for my entire life, and I had to do it immediately! I was again at that same moment of decision.

The ranger suggested that I wait for the ambulance. But I couldn't imagine waiting that long to get to a hospital. I released myself from the ranger's care, took a deep breath, walked out to my truck and began the solo drive to the hospital.

I reentered the twenty-one miles of rough road at a hurried pace, kicking dirt with my wheels when it was safe, and driving slowly when the road demanded caution. With every movement forward, I spoke out loud every positive affirmation and prayer I could think of. I kept visualizing myself walking into the emergency room and being immediately treated. I created the entire sequence of events in advance in my mind, and that visualization gave me the courage and clarity of thought to complete the drive. After about thirty minutes, I finally made it to the highway where I was able to pick up speed and make tracks toward the emergency room. My truck is a five-speed manual. I was using my shifting hand to keep direct pressure on my wound, so I had to use my left hand to steer and change gears.

It wasn't until I made it to the highway that I was able to regain cell phone coverage. I called my godfather, briefly described to him what had happened and asked him for directions to the Durango hospital. The eighty-mile drive was surrealistic, the longest eighty miles I have ever driven. I was so focused on my outcome and over stimulated with adrenaline that time simply stopped and I was simply moving through the emotions of hope, anticipation and uncertainty.

I finally made it to Durango, only to find out that the hospital had closed. How was this possible? How could a major mountain town not have a hospital? I finally found someone who told me that a new hospital had opened up several miles away. I was still completely filled with adrenaline, and so focused on my outcome, that it never occurred to me to ask the person to drive me there. Instead, I called the hospital, got the new address, checked myself into the emergency room and began the journey of physical, mental and emotional healing.

Lying on the emergency room table having my head and scalp scrubbed and stitched was one of the happiest moments in my life. The doctors remarked I was the first person to arrive in their emergency room with a head injury that was happy. I wasn't happy to be injured, but I was extremely happy and grateful to be alive. And after five-plus hours from the time of my injury to the operating table, I was completely happy to be there. The feeling of having my head scrubbed, and the tugging sensation on my scalp as the doctor pushed the needle and stitches through my head, was joyful...and surreal. Life has so many unexpected twists and turns. I started my day on a peaceful journey, and now I was lying on an emergency-room table practically joyful as my head was being sewn back together.

After I was released from the hospital, my friend Rich Millard took me into his Durango home. From there, another friend, Valan Cain, welcomed me into his home at Lake Vallecito. I was definitely happy and grateful to be amongst friends, and truly appreciative of their hospitality.

I didn't return to Telluride for nearly two weeks after my injury. During those weeks, as the laceration on my head mended, I made these commitments to myself: I will never again take a single moment for granted. I will rededicate my life to living in a place of laughter, love and gratitude. I will live my life in harmony with my renewed sense of purpose. I will be passionate about how I express my love, gratitude and affection toward other people and life. And I will be passionate about my dreams and goals.

FIVE

Big Love

If one dream should fall and break into a thousand pieces, never be afraid to pick one of those pieces up and begin again.

~ Flavia Weedn

NEVER IN MY LIFE was I more alive and more in the moment than the day I hiked out, my scalp split open, my body covered in my own blood, and my head spinning from a concussion. It was a transformational day that remains vividly inscribed in my mind.

Life presents so many different opportunities to learn and grow. I went to Chaco Canyon to find peace, reflection and relaxation before I went to Denver for hernia surgery. Somehow, that choice led me to a path where a rock was already destined to fall. This collision was a defining moment in my life. When the universe gives you a near-death experience, your entire perception of life changes, and you come out with a deep appreciation for life that can only be seen through the eyes of someone who has faced death.

There was a lot more to recovering from the rock fall than my physical healing. That event put my entire life in question. Had I been two inches closer to the wall, I would certainly have been killed because the rock would have landed directly on top of my head and crushed my skull. Instead, it caught the top right side of my head with enough force to jar my brain and give me a concussion and split my scalp open. The difference between life and death was only a couple of inches. Those few inches teach a valuable lesson. The distance between life and death is tiny. It doesn't take much to alter the direction of our life. Small changes right now can transform into huge differences down the road.

The day of my injury and self-rescue was both the scariest and happiest of my life. If people truly understood the value of life and recognized how wonderful, beautiful and abundant life truly is, we would no longer take a single second for granted. We would no longer waste our time on petty differences or tolerate any of the negative politics and destructive thinking and behavior that blankets our planet. We would immediately shift our attention to what is beautiful and amazing about life. Through that shift in focus, everything that is good and beautiful would expand.

The person I was before this injury is only a shadow of the person I am today. I have learned so much about life, and these words only touch upon the overall beauty of this incredible gift.

It has taken quite some time to regroup and take a deep, honest look at the life I was living before I was injured. That life was rich with experience, adventure and love. Yet, overall, it was not the life I truly wanted to live. I was doing fun things, taking risks and learning and growing through my choices and actions. But at the end of the day, there was something missing.

During the summer of 2009, a year after the rock fell on me, I was still having a difficult time. I was still feeling challenged by the residual effects of my concussion and I hadn't made a lot of progress clarifying how I wanted to live my life. I started reading all of my poetry and writing from times past and made a choice to dig deep into my heart and soul. I camped out in the Telluride mountains most of the summer so that I could have time to myself without day-to-day distractions. In my solitude, I began to retrace my life up until the moment of the rock fall and eventually realized what had happened: I had lost track of my sense of purpose, which at one time was very strong in my heart and mind. Without a sense of purpose, I was going through life doing things but not loving myself or what I was doing.

I gained my sense of purpose early in life through the death of my mother. When I was fifteen, my mother passed away after having been in a coma for the final year of her life. When she was diagnosed with a brain tumor, and subsequently died two years later from the failed radiation therapy, my entire family went into a tailspin and fell apart. The family drama became emotionally unmanageable. I could no longer handle the fighting amongst my relatives, and I could no longer handle the pain and rejection that grew out of my mother's death and all the resultant bickering.

For a short period after my mother died, I lived with my stepfather and his new wife. Although she loved my stepfather, she resented me. I was the son of his deceased wife, and she wanted no part of me. I would hear her scream and yell at night, telling my stepfather that he had to choose either me or her, but that he couldn't have both. That became the last straw in my emotional tolerance. I could no longer handle her deep rejection and hatred. I knew that if I didn't leave, I would self-destruct. So at sixteen, I moved out on my own — from Great Neck, New York to Telluride. The day that I made that choice was one of the happiest of my life because it freed me from the emotional venom of my past.

Even though my mother was dead, I kept her very much alive in my heart. And her love became the driving force behind my will to survive and persevere. I worked full-time while putting myself through high school and college and have been moving forward ever since. Along the way there have been a handful of people who took me under their wing, adopted me into their lives and treated me like family. One of the people I met was a Wizard named Hawkwind who I refer to as my Godfather. Through the best and worst of times, each of these people loved me, guided me and supported me in a way that is angelic.

As a result of the incredible love and goodness that I was blessed with, I gained a clear sense of purpose and made a promise to myself that, somehow, I would return the favor by touching the heart of every person I met and making a positive difference in the world. I didn't know how to do it. Yet I knew that it would have to be done in order to continue the cycles of love and contribution.

Living on my own in Telluride in the 1980s was not as difficult as I had first anticipated. The small community was very loving and supportive. Going to college at the University of Colorado at Boulder was a bit more challenging, though, not because of the size of the university or the caliber of the classes but because of the emotional challenge of feeling like an orphan with no family structure to support or encourage me. I was truly blessed by the people who had adopted me into their lives during high school. But the college environment magnified my emotional displacement. Parents' weekend and the holidays were very difficult. My commitment to working through this challenge was driven by my love for my mother and by my desire to return the favor of goodness that was extended to me. Through my passion for contribution, I sought out people, adventures and organizations that would help me to grow as a person and also give me some semblance of a family structure. I did the best I could to create my own sense of self-worth by immersing myself in the sports and fitness lifestyle and by joining social organizations that added needed structure to my life and gave me a creative outlet for social and community contribution.

Somewhere along the way, several years after I graduated from college, I unknowingly began to lose touch with my sense of purpose, and my life slowly moved in a direction counter to what I really wanted to accomplish. This unhealthy tangent grew from deep roots of self-doubt that had been eating away at my belief in myself and in my dreams. I sought out answers by attending personal-development seminars and broadening my understanding of basic human needs and social conditioning. Everything I learned was wonderful and has contributed tremendously to my understanding of life. Yet at my core, there were still deep tears hiding behind my eyes and I didn't know how to release them.

During my recovery, a lot of people commented that it must have been very bad luck to get hit by a rock. I don't believe in luck. Luck is nothing more than a word to describe circumstances that we don't understand. If anything, this dance with the rock has been the greatest blessing I have ever received because it was the catalyst that released my tears, woke me up and brought me back in touch with my true purpose in life. Sharing my story is my first big step in that direction.

Nearly two years have passed since my collision with destiny. In that time I have learned far more about people, life, love and myself than I ever could have imagined. Harvesting the lessons from this experience has been one of the greatest challenges I have ever faced. Yet facing it has been the most rewarding journey I have ever travelled. The biggest reward was when I became clear on what I wanted to do with my life from that point forward. Yet making that leap from knowing to actually doing took a lot of quiet time and reflection and didn't come without some resistance. It's exciting to know what you want to do with your life. But it can also be scary taking that first step. Fortunately, I'm not alone. There is an entire universe to provide support and encouragement.

Each day of our lives we pass hundreds if not thousands of people who we will never meet or get close to. We may share a smile, a wink or a nod, but that's as far as it goes. Every so often, though, our paths cross with someone whose energy, interests and emotions magnetically blend with our own and, through that energetic attraction, we form a refreshingly new friendship, our life blossoms, and we experience a whole new level of life.

On May 26th, 2010 I met such a person and I received a huge boost of inspiration. On this magical day, the universe unexpectedly brought into my life an incredibly talented, creative, loving, caring, compassionate soul. Our friendship grew very quickly in a short period of time. Through the example of his own life and the sincere way he expressed his love and friendship toward everyone, Matt Drews inspired me to take the leap that would complete this book and bring to form the sharing of the gift of this experience.

Matt's favorite expression is Big Love! When he hugs you, you feel like you've been hugged by the entire universe. When he smiles, the whole sky lights up. If one person can make that much of a difference in people's lives simply by smiling, hugging and being authentic, then I have to believe that the lessons of my experience can also spread Big Love and can inspire others to heal themselves and brighten our world.

BIG love
Oceans of Love.
Everywhere I Look, I See Oceans of Love.
High Tide — Low Tide.
Love is Everywhere.
In the Waters, In The Skies, On The Land.
Love Is Here — Love Is There.
It Is Within Our Hearts
And Joys In Being Shared.
I Give To You My Oceans.
I Give To You — MY love.
~ David Lloyd Strauss

...Map and Photos

To thine own self be true, and it must follow, as the night the day,
thou canst not then be false to any man.
~ William Shakespeare

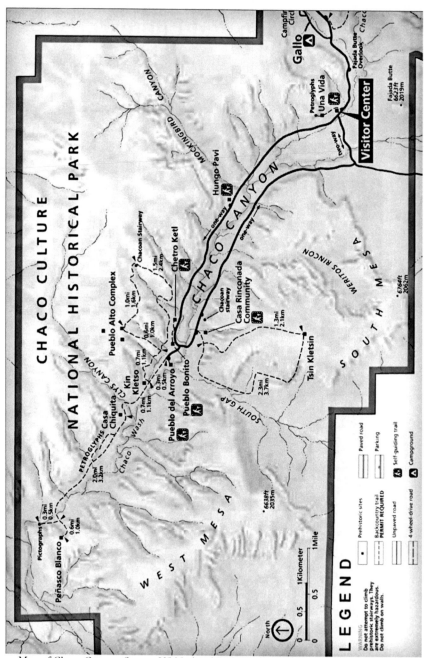

Map of Chaco Canyon: Source US National Park Service Website: www.nps.gov/chcu

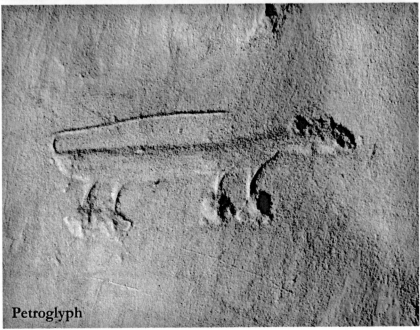

Petroglyph

Large Kiva

Small Kivas

Pueblo Bonito Overlook

Crack Canyon

Approximately two hours before my injury

BOOK TWO

I *believe that you're great, that there's something magnificent about you. Regardless of what has happened to you in your life, regardless of how young or how old you think you might be, the moment you begin to think properly, this something that is within you, this power within you that's greater than the world, it will begin to emerge. It will take over your life. It will feed you, it will clothe you, it will guide you, protect you, direct you, sustain your very existence. If you let it! Now that is what I know, for sure.*

~ Michael Beckwith

SIX

The Student Is Ready

Watch your thoughts, for they become words.
Watch your words, for they become actions.
Watch your actions, for they become habits.
Watch your habits, for they become character.
Watch your character, for it becomes your destiny.
~ Unknown

WHEN I WAS A CHILD, my father introduced me to health, fitness and wellness. He told me that living a healthy and fit lifestyle is the most valuable gift you can give to yourself. Having full access to all your senses is the most delicious snack imaginable. Nothing in the world tastes as delicious as being healthy, fit and vibrant feels. There is nothing more fulfilling and rewarding than being able to immerse yourself in the activities of life: to be able to run, bike, swim, climb mountains, watch a rainbow, follow a butterfly with your eyes or feel the tingle of a ladybug on your arm. The richest experience in the world is to laugh with the full depth of your lungs, to smile with open jowls of joy and to have the energy to help yourself and others.

In simple words, he told me that everything you allow into your body affects your physical, mental and emotional health. If you don't take care of your body, you have nowhere else to live. Once you lose your health, you have lost access to all that life has to offer. He is now 84 years young and still lives a vibrant, active life filled with love and laughter. Through his example, I have been healthy and physically fit all my life. My father is a truly unique person. He is a true master of energy health and vitality!

Although I have done quite a bit to stay healthy, my love for extreme sports and adventure has given me my fair share of injuries. My body has been through a lot and it's been very good to me. But I've never had an injury that impacted my life as physically and emotionally as the one that resulted from that rock fall.

Being deprived of physical activity was, for me, the near equivalent of being deprived of air. When you're accustomed to living at the peak of your senses and you suddenly lose that ability for nearly a year, your whole life goes into a tailspin. My scalp healed quickly, but my concussion definitely added a whole new twist to my life. Anyone who has had a concussion, or knows someone who has had one, understands the comedy of errors resulting from all the headaches and forgetfulness. It would have been a lot more fun if I could have chosen what to forget. But no such luck. I forgot things at random, which definitely stirred up a variety of troubles. The memory deficits and headaches continued for over a year, then slowly subsided. The real adventure was going in for hernia surgery six weeks after my head injury. The combination of my concussion and recovering from surgery made for a very interesting two years. The pain from my hernia surgery was like getting kicked in the groin by an elephant. Imagine lying in bed and forgetting why you have so much pain down there. Ugh!

During the time of my combined recovery, many questions entered my mind about the meaning of life. When you have a near-death experience and then spend most of the next year recovering from a concussion and double-hernia surgery, you have a lot of time to think. Given that I'd had two severe injuries simultaneously, it was difficult for me to fall into conventional thinking and believe that this was just bad luck. I prefer to believe that there is a lot more order in the universe than just random events, and I wanted to explore the full depth of this idea.

When I looked at where I had been emotionally at that point in my life, and at all the thoughts that had been going through my head just before the rock hit me, I couldn't accept that this was simply an unfortunate coincidence. The tone of my thoughts during that hike were boiling with frustration, anxiety and disillusionment about the direction of my life and the overall condition of our world. I was more focused on problems rather than solutions. I felt out of alignment, and perhaps all this had to happen to wake me up and shift my focus. Which it did. My wake-up was slow and steady. I had a lot of physical, mental and emotional healing to go through. The hernia surgery was definitely the most painful, but the combination of the two was a bit over the top.

One evening while lying in bed, I remember thinking that I only had two choices when it came to my healing. I could take the "blue pill" and take the easy way out, allowing my body to heal without actually learning anything. Or I could take the "red pill" and explore the deeper meaning of this experience. The reality was that I had been given a second chance at life. Given that, there was no way I was going to continue with the same beliefs and level of thinking that had brought me to that transitional point in time. My near-death experience demanded that I ask different questions about life. And I did. The first person I spoke with was Hawkwind.

Ever since I first met Hawkwind when I was 16, he has been a powerful guide in my life. When I approached him about the journey of healing from this injury, he reminded me that life is a classroom. We are all teachers and students for each other, and our experiences are our lessons in disguise. He told me that all healing starts in the mind. In order to heal our body, he said, we first have to heal our mind. If we don't heal our mind, the same lessons will continue to show up in our lives, but disguised as different experiences. He made it very clear to me that my body is well-equipped to do most of the physical healing, and that my energies were best focused on learning the true nature of the mind and healing my mind.

Clearly, Hawkwind was correct. My mind needed healing. It took the equivalent of a kick in the groin and a knock on the head to stop me in my tracks and get me to notice. It also meant that I had a lot to learn because if all healing starts in the mind, I did not have a clear understanding of what the mind is, nor how it works on a day-by-day, moment-by-moment basis.

My journey of healing my mind started with my thoughts about gravity. Clearly it was the law of gravity that had dropped the rock onto my head. But was there also a law that had brought my head in contact with the rock? Were there other laws of life that worked harmoniously to bring our parallel paths together? Was there any relationship between what I had been thinking and what had happened to me? If all healing starts in the mind, I wondered, then what is the mind?

By asking these questions and inquiring into the deeper cause of my injuries, I started to draw into my life the people and circumstances that would reveal to me the very issues I was seeking to understand. As I collected various ideas and perceptions, some familiar and some new, it felt as though the truth and understanding that I was seeking was scattered like a jigsaw puzzle that I was trying to piece together with one eye blindfolded and one hand tied behind my back. My entire path shifted away from physical healing. Instead, I launched into a mini-course of discovery into the natural laws of life and the nature of the human mind so that I could overcome my own mental and emotional limitations.

I already knew about the law of attraction. Yet I wasn't familiar with the depth to which it operates. I also wasn't satisfied with the possibility of there being only two laws holding the universe together: the laws of gravity and attraction. I wanted to know all the natural laws that control everything around us and that weave the web of life. My rescue mission would not be over until I was totally healed, which couldn't happen until I understood those laws and was able to share what I had learned.

There is an old saying that seemed appropriate for me at that point in time: "When the student is ready, the teacher will appear." I was ready! I was ready for new ideas and a fresh way of looking at life.

I believe very strongly in the value of mentoring. If you want something in life, find someone who has what you want, learn from them and follow in their footsteps. Strong mentors can not only teach you what they know, they can guide you in healthy and meaningful ways when you're off track. As Hawkwind once taught me, there are many different areas to life: physical, spiritual, mental, emotional, family, career, community, social and financial. And we can have mentors in each of those areas. If we don't learn through mentors, we will learn vicariously through experience, which can be slow and costly. Choosing the right mentor is very important because this is someone you will be learning from and modeling after in order to achieve an outcome. Choosing the wrong mentor can put you down the wrong path and waste precious time and opportunity.

Being selective about whose opinion and advice we listen to and follow is very important. People are not always what they say they are. Some are better than they say. Others are only shadows of how they present themselves. The only way to measure truth of character is by the results that show up in a person's life. I'm not talking about financial results. I'm talking about overall results. I'm talking about results of character. We all have weaknesses in our character and we all make mistakes that we can learn and grow from. But be wary of the Wizard of Oz: the big voice that is really only a small man with a microphone hiding behind a curtain. If your mentor's life is not consistent with what he is saying, if she speaks one way and acts another, then run in the other direction...and run fast. If you find mentors whose lives are consistent with their words, then grab onto their coattails!

I have had many wonderful mentors in my life who have helped me to gain a broad understanding of human relations. They have also helped me build a strong foundation toward a healthy, vibrant and active lifestyle. Among them are Anthony Robbins, Dale Carnegie, Earl Nightingale, Jack Canfield, James Allen, Napoleon Hill, Norman Vincent Peale, Og Mandino, and Paramahansa Yogananda. Each has shared unique tools and perceptions based on similar truths and has been invaluable when it comes to shaping my character, relating with others, overcoming obstacles and living a deep and meaningful life. Yet with all the knowledge, wisdom and awareness they had conveyed, my quest to understand the nature of the mind would require a new mentor who could answer my very specific questions.

Through my two injuries, it became very apparent to me that there was a clear disparity between what I had learned, and the overall quality of my life. I had learned a lot of valuable life skills from my mentors, yet I still had self-destructive patterns of thinking that had led not only to these two injuries but also to earlier injuries and difficulties. I felt as though I had been taught the answers to my questions in bits and pieces, but they didn't form one cohesive set of thoughts and beliefs. It was as if an invisible wall prevented me from integrating all that I had learned into my actual day-to-day life. This wall was the barricade that I kept bumping into, the wall that had brought the injuries and difficulties into my life.

If I wanted to learn and grow from my experience, while at the same time healing my mind and body, I would have to figure out what I don't know, and learn it. I would have to expand my awareness about what my mind is and how it works in concert with my body. I wasn't looking for textbook answers. I wanted answers from mentors whose lives demonstrated what they know and teach. I wasn't interested in learning from someone who was simply repeating other people's ideas or who was a Wizard of Oz. I was only interested in someone who could explain the laws of life, the mind, and how they work together to shape my life. I wanted mentors who were truly in touch with their own minds and bodies, as reflected in the quality of their health, friendships and relationships and overall quality of life.

Surprisingly, one of the people I stumbled upon was someone I was already familiar with from the movie The Secret. Bob Proctor, for me, was one of the most powerful figures in that movie. Yet I hadn't realized that he was a world-renowned authority on the human mind and the natural laws of the universe. He was exactly the person I was looking for. I immediately chose him as a mentor and became a student of his teachings.

Bob himself is a lifelong student of the greatest nineteenth- and twentieth-century teachers of the relationship between thought, emotion and things: Napoleon Hill, Wallace D. Wattles, Earl Nightingale and Andrew Carnegie. Although Bob wasn't the one who discovered the natural laws of the universe or how the mind works, he is a master student and teacher. He has the incredible ability to distill ancient wisdom and the wisdom of the greatest minds into a mental tonic that is easily understood and easily integrated into life. He has a strong and intentional voice and incredible clarity of thought and purpose. And he shares his understandings with the same care and delicate strength that a butler would use in carrying the finest piece of crystal.

The Secret was one of the top movies of 2007, entering the hearts and minds of humanity across the globe like a ferocious firestorm. It's a fantastic presentation about the law of attraction. However, in Bob Proctor's first full line in the movie he implied that there is more than one law.

We all work with one infinite power. We all guide ourselves by exactly the same laws. The natural laws of the universe are so precise that we don't even have any difficulty building spaceships. We can send people to the moon, and we can time the landing within the fraction of a second. ~ Bob Proctor

In order to fully grasp the gift of a second chance at life, I wanted to know not only what laws he was referring to, but how to use them. If this injury was a dress rehearsal for my own death, I wanted to know how I drew this experience into my life and how I could use those laws with definiteness of purpose for the remainder of my life. I also wanted to know and understand what the mind is and how to use it with that same definiteness of purpose.

What Bob teaches is simple. Our experience of life is not what we think it is. Nothing in the world is as it appears. The world in which we live, our everyday life, the reality that we see, taste, touch and smell, is only one layer of a reality that is far greater than we could ever imagine with our physical senses. There is nothing random about life. There are no coincidences. We live in an orderly universe bound together by one great law, the law of energy, and by its seven subsidiary laws: the seven natural laws of the universe. The dance of life, along with all its acts, scenes, and charades, is driven by these laws.

Everything that happens to us, within us and amongst us is occurring by law. These seven laws govern how life relates to itself and determine all our experiences. Gaining an applied awareness and understanding of these laws can wash away all the uncertainty and doubt. It's the map to the treasure chest of life. The key to the treasure chest is disguised as one emotion that is the foundation for activating the full potential of these laws.

Each of the seven laws work together with harmony, accuracy and precision to create the entire experience of life. They are laws. We cannot turn them on or off. They operate whether we are aware of them or not. They govern the entire universe; they also govern every area of our daily lives. How we work with these laws, whether we are aware of them or not, governs the quality of our health, our relationships, our finances. It governs everything, right down to our day-to-day, minute-by-minute experiences.

My first look into the laws astounded me. I had been anticipating long, drawn-out, detailed descriptions of how life works. I was preparing myself for the study of these laws in much the same way a student would prepare to study law at a university. I was expecting to see volumes of books and untold references to each possibility of life. To my surprise, the laws themselves consisted of only a few simple words. Yet the depth of their power extended across the entire tapestry of time. It would be easy to be fooled by their simplicity. But the reality is that even though they are but a few words, they require you to completely abandon all preconceived thoughts about life and to open yourself up to an entirely new world of possibilities. When I first started studying them, they felt intuitively correct. At the same time, they were emotionally challenging. To truly embrace them took a level of emotional vulnerability and honesty that I hadn't faced in quite some time.

With all their simplicity, the seven laws are powerful enough to shape our entire life experience.

- ❖ The Law of Vibration / Attraction
- ❖ The Law of Cause and Effect
- ❖ The Law of Polarity
- ❖ The Law of Relativity
- ❖ The Law of Rhythm
- ❖ The Law of Transmutation of Energy
- ❖ The Law of Gender

To study the laws and ignore the study of what the mind is and how it works would be the equivalent of deciding you don't want to skydive halfway through your jump. They are each interconnected and play a common role in shaping our lives. To understand the mind is to understand the seven laws. To understand the seven laws is to understand the mind.

Most people think of the mind as our brain. It's not. The brain is part of the body and our body an instrument of the mind. There are two parts to our mind: our conscious mind and our subconscious mind. Both work together with the body to shape our personality and create our life experiences.

Our conscious mind is the place where we think and reason. It's also the place where we interact with the outside world through our five senses of taste, touch smell, hearing and sight. This is the place where ideas of pleasure, pain, poverty, limitation, abundance or lack originate. Since we have the ability to think and reason, it is through our conscious mind and through our own free will that we have complete control over which ideas we accept or reject. Our conscious mind is a gatekeeper, a filter to our subconscious mind.

Our subconscious mind is the power center for our entire experience of life. It operates in every cell of our body. It operates in an orderly manner and, by law, expresses itself through our feelings and actions. It's the recipient of the thoughts, ideas and beliefs that we have first accepted into our conscious mind. Anything that is allowed and accepted into our subconscious mind becomes a part of our overall system of beliefs, habits and behaviors and thus shapes and influences all of our life experiences. Any thought that we continuously impress upon our subconscious mind becomes a part of our personality and beliefs.

The thoughts in our conscious mind are like seeds, and our subconscious mind is like the soil. We can either choose our own thoughts or we can accept them from an outside source. Whatever we allow into our conscious and subconscious minds will be expressed through our body and our senses as our experiences of life.

When we are having a conversation with a person, we are not talking with their face. We are talking with the filter of their conscious mind and the beliefs of their subconscious mind. We, as humans, do not think in words. We think in pictures. We can create an image in our mind of almost anything of a material or tangible nature. But we don't have a picture of our mind because our mind is not a thing. Mind is the activity of consciousness. It is the energy of thought.

In 1934 Dr. Thurman Fleet of San Antonio, Texas developed a simple diagram to demonstrate the conscious and subconscious mind, and the body.

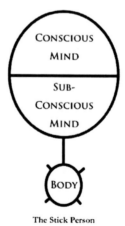

The Stick Person

The big circle represents our head and the smaller circle represents our body. Our mind is not limited to our head. Mind is in everything. It is in our head, through our brain, that we think with our mind. The three elements of our conscious and subconscious mind, and our body create our personality and the totality of our life experiences.

This diagram was first introduced to me by Bob Proctor. It has been a very practical tool in helping me to visualize what the mind is. And, it has also been enormously useful in understanding how to utilize the relationship between the conscious and subconscious mind and our body.

Just as we have five senses of taste, touch, smell, sight and hearing that allow us to interact with our environment, there are six faculties to the human mind that allow us to interact with life. Each of these faculties, individually and collectively, is a powerful force in the happenings of life.

The faculties of the mind:

- ❖ Will
- ❖ Memory
- ❖ Perception
- ❖ Reason
- ❖ Intuition
- ❖ Imagination

Once I discovered the six faculties of the mind and the seven natural laws of the universe, I studied them ferociously and found myself with an entirely new perspective on life. Not only did I make peace with my injuries, I began to make peace with every calamity in my past.

My next step would be to return to Chaco Canyon to bring this entire experience into perspective and turn it into something valuable and meaningful for myself and others. On August 22nd, 2010, through my renewed courage and inspiration, I returned to Chaco to pay homage to the rock, and to begin the next stage of my journey of bringing this story to the world.

SEVEN

Desert Oasis

There is a breath and pulse of life that beats to the drums of the dance we call
"Self". This dance is a dance of laws, and it truly is a dance.
~ David Lloyd Strauss

O N MY RETURN JOURNEY to Chaco Canyon, I followed the same
route through Telluride, Rico, Dolores and Durango. Throughout
the entire drive, my eyes were pooling with tears and the knot in my belly
echoed the volume of my anxiety. Once I finally pulled onto the dirt road
that leads to Chaco Culture National Historical Park, I paused often to
breathe in the desert air and shake off my tension. A few miles before the
main entrance, I noticed an incredible ocean of fresh desert sage. I pulled
over, stepped out of my truck and walked to the edge of that aromatic
oasis. I took a deep breath, and my lungs and senses were tickled with joy
and rejuvenation. The air was saturated with one of the most pleasant,
healing refreshing scents imaginable.

Since ancient times — as far back as the ancient Celts, Druids, Hindus,
Buddhists and Catholic and Eastern Orthodox churches — sage has been
used for healing, purification and protection, and to increase knowledge and
wisdom. In Native American traditions, sage is used during cleansing rituals
in kivas and sweat lodges. As I looked out across that oasis, I imagined the

Anasazi harvesting sage from this very area for use in their many cultural ceremonies.

I was first introduced to sage at age sixteen during my early years in Telluride, when I met a group of modern-day wizards. These heart- and healing-centered mountain folk, "keepers of ancient wisdom," shared with me the experience of traditional sweat lodges, as well as other powerful ceremonies and dances.

Through my memory of that experience, and knowing that this would be a day of healing and wisdom for me, I gave thanks to mother earth for showing me this magical oasis. I then gathered some sage to bring with me onto my journey of inner and outer reflection.

I returned to my truck and drove to the main entrance. Once again, I pulled over and began my ceremonial entrance into a place and time that had transformed my life. Sage in hand, I stepped from the truck, walked over to the grand entrance and placed four small bundles of sage on the sign, with each of the bundles pointing in one of the four sacred directions (East, West, North, South). I then rubbed one small branch of sage into my hands and covered my arms, legs, face, head and neck with the pure, fresh essence of this delightful gift from the desert. Holding a fifth bundle, I offered a prayer of love and gratitude to open my heart and mind, and to set my intention for the day ahead.

Great Spirit of Light and Love, thank you for returning me to the place of my spiritual and emotional death and rebirth. Thank you for this time of reflection as I gather the words and wisdom to awaken the power of this experience, and the gift that will flow through this journey.

After a moment of silence, feeling the tears in my eyes and heart, I returned to my truck, placed the fifth bundle of sage in my back pack to carry with me throughout the day, turned on solo bamboo-flute music and reentered the canyon.

First, I drove one full loop around the entire park to honor the spirits and to refresh my memory of my earlier journey. Everything seemed familiar but ever so far away. Even though it had been barely two years earlier since I had danced with the energy of the rock, in my own heart and mind, it had been many lifetimes ago.

A strong part of me wanted to pick up where I had left off and see the sights I'd missed the last time. I resisted the temptation and chose to stay true to the intention of my journey, driving straight to the Pueblo Alto parking area to commence my return to the mirror of my past. When I arrived at the registration post to fill out my hiking permit, there were three college students joking about the registration form. I joined in on their laugh for a moment, then told them my story. I pointed out that had I not made it down on my own by nightfall, that "silly little permit" would have been the only message to the world that I was still up there, dead or alive. Their tone changed.

I filled out my permit and began my walk along the dirt path toward the crack canyon. My feet and heart were heavy. With each step, I felt both the eager anticipation of a college graduation and the solemnity of a funeral. It was an odd mix of emotions, yet an honest blend of joy and sadness. When I reached the entrance of the crack canyon, a huge explosion of tears burst through my eyes. I had very vivid memories of reaching that same point at the end of my self-rescue. It was a painful, yet joyous reflection. This time I was a lot more aware of my environment, and I brought the added safety features of a helmet and a safety whistle. After my tears calmed, I began my ascent up the rock trail and into the crack canyon. I stopped briefly between the two rock walls and wondered how I had made it through those last few hundred feet with an open head wound and a concussion. Adrenaline goes a long way when you're injured! When I finally reached the top, I felt like I had just emerged from the womb of my rebirth. My body tingled, my chest felt heavy with emotions and the drumbeat of my heart was pounding with cautious expectation. I took off my sunglasses, spread my arms into the wind, filled my lungs with the warm desert air, and replenished my heart with gratitude.

Reality set in. Two years earlier I had been clawing for my life. Now I was at the beginning of the journey of my rebirth. This was far more overwhelming than I had anticipated. I perched myself on a small rock shelf only a few steps away and looked out over the plateau. My mind wandered away from the trail in front of me, and I remembered my dream in the hall of mirrors. I remembered the strands of crystals, the harmonic tone of the crystals and the column of white light. I remembered that, in the dream, I had chosen the journey of learning who and what we are through my own near-death experience, and the experience of my self-rescue. I shook my head in wonder and refocused on the trail ahead. What I saw again filled my eyes with tears: the entire cycle of life was laid out in front of me as one simple and beautiful image in nature. The sun beat down on the rocks. The rocks absorbed heat into the earth and radiated the warmth into the air, creating the illusion of a desert oasis. Clouds moved across the sky and a light breeze swept dust across the land. In the far background, rain clouds dropped rain on the desert, while thunder and lightning filled the air. As the sun pressed through the clouds, the moisture in the air became a natural filter and made each individual ray of light visible to the naked eye, casting a rainbow of colors across the desert sky. It was the most magical cycle of giving and receiving.

As I sat there absorbing the heat with my body and watching the illusion of the oasis, I realized how simple life had become. The greatest gift I ever received was in thinking that my life had ended because, now, I understood the value of life, the laws of life and the secret to life. The experience had been worth every moment of fear, pain, uncertainty, discomfort and inconvenience because the truths I had discovered were the tools for making dreams come true.

Everything I had learned came down to one simple truth. It was something I was introduced to many years earlier but, until now, had never fully grasped. Understanding this truth brought the entire rock experience into perspective and transformed every area of my life. The heat radiating off the rock, creating the illusion of an oasis was the perfect visual image of this truth, and it set in motion my feelings and thoughts for the day.

There is one "rock-solid" indisputable truth: Everything is made of energy and everything is energetically connected. There is no separation between anyone or anything. We are all individualized expressions of the same field of energy. We each have our unique personalities and lives and our unique vibrations. Yet we are still one. This field of energy is the energy of mind. There is only one self, one heart and one mind, individualized as every expression of life. This energy, this mind, in its purest form is what some call the energy of love, infinite intelligence or God. This love-energy is the intelligence of the entire universe. It is in everything and everything is in it. It is a magical, energetic dance of endless possibilities for shapes, sizes, forms, textures, tastes, colors and sounds. The entire field of energy, in all its forms, is expressed in the physical world according to the seven natural laws of energy.

Everything is energy! Our thoughts are energy. Our feelings are energy. Our surroundings are energy. All animals and everything in nature are made of energy. Our bodies are a field of energy within a larger field of energy. All things tangible and intangible are made of energy. Everything that we experience through our senses and perception is a reflection of this energy. In any given moment, everything we experience through our senses appears separate. Yet the truth is that there is no separation. There are differences among us and between us. But there is no separation. Each person and every entity is connected through a continuous field of energy. The energy that lights the sun is the same energy that creates the sun. The energy that creates the clouds and the rain is the same energy that creates the thunder and lightning. The energy that creates you is the same energy that creates me. All of life is energetically connected. Everything is unique but the same. Everything is connected to everything. Nothing stands alone. Everything is a part of the whole. We cannot pollute the ocean and not pollute our bodies. We cannot harm someone else without harming part of ourselves. We cannot receive without being given to. We cannot exhale without inhaling. And cannot love another without loving ourselves. We are both the giver and the receiver, the creative and receptive.

The wave is the same as the ocean, though it is not the whole ocean. So each wave of creation is a part of the eternal Ocean of Spirit. The Ocean can exist without the waves, but the waves cannot exist without the Ocean.
~ *Paramahansa Yogananda*

Everything is made of the same energy. Yet it is the law of vibration that shapes the differences in the way things appear. This law is quite simple. Energy is always in motion. Everything moves. Nothing is at rest. Everything that can be seen, tasted, touched or smelled has its own frequency, and its own unique signature of vibration. Everything is dancing its own dance. The way things appear is based on their rate of vibration. The sun vibrates at a different frequency than the moon, and the moon vibrates differently than a flower or a song. As the wind blows and whistles between two rocks, it creates a vibration of sound. Every string on a guitar plays a different tone because each string is designed to vibrate differently. We have music because musicians have learned how to play with the different frequencies. Our words and thoughts are no different than the strings on a guitar. And the results in our life are like the music coming off the strings of our thoughts, feelings and actions.

The law of vibration is akin to the law of attraction. Put simply, all energy has magnetic force. Like attracts like. "Birds of a feather flock together." Energies of like vibration attract each other. The higher the frequency of vibration, the more powerful the force will be. Thought is considered to be the highest form of vibration, with the highest frequency. Therefore, thought is considered the most powerful force in the universe. Each thought, feeling and belief carries a unique vibration. We can have positive or negative thoughts. Positive thoughts create positive vibrations.

Negative thoughts create negative vibrations. When use the word "feeling" to describe our emotions, we are describing our conscious awareness of the vibration we are in. If a person says "I am not feeling very well", what they are actually saying is "I am in a negative vibration". Likewise, when a person says "I feel great", they are saying "I am in a positive vibration"

Our thoughts are magnets. Whatever thoughts, feelings and beliefs are dancing in our mind creates a vibration – a magnetic force that will attract into our lives the people, places and circumstances that are in harmony with the vibration of those same thoughts, feelings and beliefs. When you're in a negative vibration, you're going to attract negative situations into your life. When you are in a positive vibration, you will attract positive situations.

The human mind grows and expands just like a garden. A garden will grow, whatever seeds are planted, watered, nourished, cultivated and harvested. If nothing is planted, then weeds will plant themselves. All thoughts are seeds, and our feelings and actions cultivate the seeds. If we don't choose which thoughts to sow, then weeds of negative thinking will move in and take over. In the same way that gardeners must continually pull the weeds from their garden, we must do the same with the thoughts in our mind. It takes continuous attention to weed the negative thoughts from our mind and to harvest and cultivate positive thoughts and beliefs. Just as a flower does not plant itself, our experiences in life are not something that happen to us from the outside in. The garden does not grow the earth; the earth grows the garden. Our experiences are something we plant, harvest and create from the inside out through the thoughts and feelings we consistently give energy to.

We lie in the lap of immense intelligence, which makes us organs of its activity and receivers of its truth. The experiences of our life are a precise mirror of the music that is coming from the strings of our words, thoughts and actions. Our instrument is our heart and mind.

~ Ralph Waldo Emerson

When we look at our lives on a moment-by-moment basis, the law of vibration is the foundation to understanding the remaining six laws. All these laws are demonstrated in the gardens of nature. The Chinese bamboo tree is a perfect example of the laws of nature, and the perfect analogy for understanding the cycle of thoughts becoming things.

Very few people are familiar with the Chinese bamboo, yet it is one of the most fascinating trees known. Once its seed is planted, it takes approximately five years for it to take root and begin to grow. The moment it makes it past the five-year mark, it grows to an astonishing ninety feet in only six weeks. What's unique about this tree is that it requires continual love and attention to grow. It has to be watered and fertilized every day without fail for five years before it can even take root. If the watering and fertilization is stopped for even a single day, it can die.

Everything grows in its own time. Everything grows according to the law of gender. All seeds have an incubation and gestation period. Everything in nature takes its own predetermined amount of time to move into reality. This includes thoughts. Each thought is a seed. And just like the Chinese bamboo needs consistent attention to grow, so too must our thoughts be incubated with consistent feelings and actions before they can take form. People who are indecisive or are always changing their mind have a difficult time growing their dreams into reality because thought-seeds cannot take root if the thoughts, feelings and actions are always changing. There is tremendous power in making and following through with decisions.

The difference between things in nature and human thoughts is that we know the incubation period for most of nature. But the incubation period for thoughts can't be known because each thought is unique and will have its own incubation period, depending on what is being manifested. What is known about human thoughts is that consistency of thought and emotion speeds up the incubation period. The law of gender suggests that since everything manifests in its own allotted time, it is a mistake to judge conditions based on appearances. Just because we don't see signs of the result showing right now doesn't mean that nothing is germinating and taking root. Nothing is as it appears because something is always incubating and in the process of becoming reality. One of the biggest mistakes is to make decisions based upon the way things appear in the moment, rather than on the outcome we desire.

The daily watering, nourishing and nurturing of the Chinese bamboo tree demonstrates the importance of being consistent with our thoughts, emotions and beliefs. This process is also an example of the law of transmutation of energy. The water and nutrients, by themselves, do not create the Chinese bamboo, but when combined with the seed of the tree and consistent nurturing, they transmute into a Chinese bamboo. Whether it is the bamboo or anything else in nature, everything contributes to everything. Everything is in the process of becoming something else. The wind plants the seed. The seed becomes a tree. The leaves fall off the tree and become soil to provide nourishment for the tree. All thoughts are in the process of becoming things. When we think, we are creating images in our mind. When we nourish these images with consistent feelings and actions, they move through us and become the conditions, circumstances and results in our life. Energy is always moving through form, into form and out of form.

Does the Chinese bamboo take five years to grow or six weeks? If you go only by what you see, it appears to take six weeks. But if you consider the years of nurturing, it takes five years. This is the law of relativity. How we see things, and the meaning we give to our experiences, is relative to our thoughts, beliefs and perception. What is slow to one person is quick to another. What is painful to one person is liberating to another. One person's trash is another person's treasure. Everything is relative to our perception and beliefs. We see things not as they are, but as we think possible based on our own beliefs. Everything has the meaning we give it.

There is rhythm to life. Everything in nature has a pulse, and a beat, an in and an out. When we see the sun rise and the sun set, when we see the tide go in and out, we are seeing the law of rhythm. Flowers open and close because of the law of rhythm. Everything in life grows harmoniously according to the law of rhythm. Everything has a natural flow and cycle. Likewise, just as everything has its own flow, the law of polarity states that everything exists in terms of its opposite. Everything has an equal and exact opposite. Light and dark. On and off. Male and female. Up and down. If something can be good, it can also be bad. If we lose something, we also gain something. Whenever we face a challenge in life, it must also mean there is an opportunity. When difficult things happen to us, the sooner we can look for the "hidden" goodness of the event, the quicker we can transmute it into something useful and meaningful.

The Chinese bamboo, as with everything in nature, is a product of the law of cause and effect. We reap what we sow, both in nature and in the mind. We sow with our thoughts and actions. Energy flows where our attention goes. Our beliefs determine our reality because our beliefs form our thoughts and actions and, together, these create our reality. The law of cause and effect is always in action. For everything we think or do, there is always a corresponding effect.

Thought and character are one, and as character can only manifest and discover itself through environment and circumstance, the outer conditions of a person's life will always be found to be harmoniously related to his inner state. This does not mean that a man's circumstances at any given time are an indication of his entire character, but that those circumstances are so intimately connected with some vital thought-element within himself that, for the time being, they are indispensable to his development.
~ James Allen

Every thought is a seed. Our thought-seeds are nourished with our feelings and actions. The more consistent we are with the images and feelings we hold in our mind, the quicker these thoughts will become things. Whatever we nourish, grows. People who consistently think about and focus on their problems, on what they are afraid of, or don't want, are actually planting, watering and nourishing the "thought seeds" of what they don't want. As a result, their life is a garden littered with experiences, the weeds, of their "don't wants." People who are afraid of going financially broke, who focus on lack, limitation and poverty, live in lack, limitation and poverty. People who are afraid of being rejected, or fear loss of love, live in rejection. People who focus on or are afraid of illness or disease, become ill or diseased. People who focus on happiness, health and abundance, live happy, healthy and abundant lives.

Life gives us everything we focus on based on the cycle of laws. These laws are always in operation whether we are aware of them or not. There is no allowance for ignorance or misunderstanding. Being aware of these laws allows us to check in with our own thoughts and feelings to preview the experiences we are sowing and soon to be harvesting. Being aware also allows us to live life with greater intention because by choosing the thoughts and beliefs that we want to focus on, we give energy to what we desire.

EIGHT

The Scarecrow

Emancipate yourselves from mental slavery.
None but ourselves can free our minds.
~ *Bob Marley*

IT WAS EASY FOR ME TO SEE how everything is made of the same energy and that everything is energetically connected. But what really caught my attention was when I grasped the truth that the rock had very little to do with my head injury. I couldn't manifest a rock fall because I wasn't even thinking about a rock fall. However, based on the laws of vibration and attraction, I had attracted an experience that was consistent with my overall thoughts and emotions at that time. The vibrations of my thoughts aligned me with an experience that brought about the answers to my questions. I could have been anywhere and, with those thoughts and emotions, some type of experience would have manifested.

It all comes down to our mind and the big gray blob between our ears: our brain. When the scarecrow from The Wizard of Oz sang "If I only had a brain," I wonder if he really knew what he was asking for. Was he asking for a brain or a mind? They are different but very much related. If we truly understood the power of our brain and mind and knew how to use them, things would be very different on this planet. I didn't realize that until I almost lost my mind...and then "rediscovered" it through this experience.

Through our brain and mind, we are connected to a universal powerhouse of unimaginable proportions. This powerhouse is the infinite reservoir of the creative love-energy of the heart of universal intelligence. Through our brain and mind, we are all walking around with incredible gifts that could bring us untold levels of health, happiness and prosperity. The problem is, we have no idea what they are or how to use them. It's the equivalent of getting a winning lottery ticket and never cashing it in.

Let's start with the big gray blob. Our brains are not just multi-terabyte hard drives for memories and minor interruptions of thinking. They're actually highly sophisticated and extraordinarily powerful electrical instruments which transform electrical frequency from one frequency of vibration to another. The information that we receive into our brain through our five senses results in muscular movement or other actions of our body or organs. Our brains are also highly sophisticated and extraordinarily powerful transmitting and receiving devices designed for the exchange and creation of thought. In the same way a cell phone can transmit and receive voice and data through the air, so too does our brain tune in to the energetic vibration of thought. There are billions of thoughts going through the air all the time. Since every thought has its own unique vibration, our brains have the messy job of tuning in and picking up the thought and emotional signals that align with our thought and emotional vibrations. We also transmit our thought signals outwardly in the same way a radio station broadcasts its signal. Basically, our brains are like thought disc jockeys, playing music (thoughts) and taking requests (receiving thoughts). When we think, we are broadcasting signals outwardly. Our audience is universal mind and infinite intelligence, which gives us feedback as the people in our lives, as emotions and experiences. We create and attract experiences (radio shows) based on our consistent thoughts, emotions and actions, and our life then becomes a mirror of the thoughts, emotions and actions that we give the most consistent energy and attention to.

Our brain is a sending-and-receiving device that works in collaboration with our mind. The brain is an organ, while the mind is a field of energy with six unique and distinct interrelated functions. These functions are the six faculties of the mind, each of which interact with our brain to create the experiences of our life. Our mind is like a giant octopus with six tentacles (which would technically make it a hexapus). The body of the octopus represents the mind; the six tentacles are the faculties of the mind, each of which works independently and collectively, playing its own role in the world of thought and form.

The first tentacle is the biggest and strongest: the tentacle of will. Our will is our ability to make choices, focus, concentrate and commit. Willpower refers to the strength of our will. Courage, loyalty, discipline and perseverance are familiar components of will. Without will, without being "willing," we would do nothing. Our personal power is our ability to use our will to choose our thoughts, beliefs and actions, and our ability to make uninhibited decisions about the direction of our life. When we surrender our personal power to others, we are releasing our ability to think for ourselves and make our own choices.

The next tentacle holds a powerful grip on the experiences of our past. It is the faculty of memory. Our memory is our ability to store and recall information. We have three types of memory: short-term, long-term and sensory. Sensory memory allows us to recognize things we have already seen. All our thoughts, beliefs and memories are stored and mapped in our brain. Every thought, belief and memory has its own set of neuro-connections in our brain that we can draw on when thinking, reflecting or creating. We actually have perfect memories. The problem is that we have not perfected our ability to recall our memories!

The third tentacle partners with the law of relativity. It is the faculty of perception. This is perhaps the trickiest of the six faculties. Our perception creates our reality. Reality does not create our perception. We actually see, feel, behave and make decisions based on what we believe. We project our beliefs, and our entire experience of life reflects back as a mirror of our thoughts and beliefs. We can only see what we believe because the brain can only see what it is mapped to see. Our brain filters out anything that does not fit into our beliefs or that it does not think is possible. When it comes to sight and sound, we don't see and hear with our eyes and ears. We see with our mind. Our eyes and ears are instruments that collect information from the outside world and deliver it to our mind, which then interprets it based on our beliefs. When we want to change our life, we first have to change our perception. We change our perception by paying attention to the relationship between thoughts, feelings, actions and results. When we change our perception of the moment, we actually change the moment.

The tentacle of reason is the faculty of the mind that we refer to as intelligence. It is through reason that we seek to find and understand truth. Inductive and deductive logic are two forms of reasoning that we use to draw conclusions from any idea, situation or premise. Imagination and reason interplay as we blend ideas to formulate conclusions.

Intuition is the invisible tentacle of insight. Think of it in terms of the internet. Google is the largest search engine on the planet, storing and exchanging remarkable amounts of information. Take all search engines together, and you would have something like a physical version of the universal mind. Not quite, though, because search engines can only store and exchange the information that we feed them. The universal mind, however, is the source and supply of all information. Intuition is a moment in time when our thoughts and feelings energetically align with a thought in the universal mind. That alignment gives us a feeling or hunch about a situation. Intuition is a form of insight...in-sight, seeing from within.

Imagination carries the highest vibration of all our faculties and is perhaps the most important. Imagination is the tentacle of creativity. To imagine is to "image-within." Everything we experience through our senses and the faculties of our mind is a reflection of imagination. Imagination is the creative use of thought. It is taking something that isn't and making it so — first in our mind, then in our reality. Imagination is what allows us to change the conditions of our life. When we create a new vision for ourselves in our mind, the seven laws of energy work cooperatively to bring the new experience into reality. When it is said that all healing starts in the mind, it is through imagining a healed body that we begin the process of healing. Albert Einstein said, "Imagination is everything. It is the preview of life's coming attractions." Napoleon Hill called imagination "the most marvelous, miraculous, inconceivably powerful force that the world has ever known."

The combination of our heart and brain, and the six faculties of our mind is a powerful force to be awakened. Together, brain and mind are magnetic, reality-creating projectors and receivers that give us access to unlimited resources and potential for shaping our life.

The combination of the thoughts in our mind and feelings in our heart is also a powerful magnetic force. It is so powerful that the consistent blending of thoughts and feelings draws the parallel experience into our reality. Whatever we consistently think about and feel, we bring about. The impact of this concept reaches far beyond conventional beliefs about emotions. Most people believe that emotions are something we feel. As I learned from Anthony Robbins, they are actually something we do. Our emotions are a feedback mechanism that tells us what we are thinking about. We do emotions because our thoughts determine our feelings and our feelings shape our behavior. Our behavior then reinforces our feelings and thoughts. Each unique thought has its own frequency of vibration that creates our feelings, and these thought-feelings show up as our emotions and body language. We link emotions to body language. If we move into body language first, we draw the emotion into our feelings. Our body language is like an on/off switch for emotions. The way a person moves will tell you everything about what he or she is thinking and feeling.

During my hike out, there were moments when I felt total despair. At other times I was full of courage. My thoughts directly impacted my behavior. The way I felt in one moment directly affected how I "showed up" in the next. When I felt fear, it was difficult to move forward because I was projecting the pain of fear, which would slow me down or stop me. When I shifted my thoughts and feelings to courage and positive expectations, I gained strength and was able to continue. My strength and movement were directly linked to my thoughts, emotions and beliefs. Each time I changed my thoughts, I changed my posture. When I was feeling courageous, I stood taller and more confident. When I was feeling fearful, I slouched and dragged.

Looking back, I realize that it was during my self-rescue that I truly became aware that we do our emotions rather than feel them. A confident person will stand, sit and move differently than a fearful one. When we align our body with our thoughts and feelings, we create a physical environment that is consistent with our feelings. It is much easier to feel courageous when we are standing tall and moving. Likewise, it is easy to feel fear or depressed when we are curled up or hunched over. One of the quickest ways to shift our emotions is to first take on the physical posture of the emotion we want to feel. If we want to feel confident, we must stand tall. Our thoughts and feelings will follow.

Our lives are molded from the thoughts, feelings and behavior that we give consistent energy and attention to. Whether we are aware of it or not, we are destined to live a life patterned after the images in our mind. We can use our thoughts to create or to destroy. Once we fully grasp this truth, and the truth that everything is energetically connected, the entire world of possibilities opens up to us. These possibilities become achievable when we understand the simple flow of energy. Change our thoughts, change our feelings. Change our feelings, change our vibrations. Change our vibrations, change our actions. Change our actions, change our reality.

We are creative, thinking, feeling creatures with unlimited power and potential to live, love and create. We have a natural-born ability to endlessly create through the use of our thoughts and imagination. Our ability to think combined with our ability to use our imagination to create original thought is our most basic asset which, when properly understood and utilized, can transform not only our individual lives but the entire direction of humanity. Our misuse of our ability to think and create can also be the source of tremendous destruction.

Everything in life offers a lesson to be learned or a truth to be remembered. The experiences of life can either draw us away or bring us closer to our own true nature. What makes the difference is the meaning we give our experiences. There is not a single event, activity or experience that does not have multiple meanings, depending on the vantage point we choose to perceive from.

Each moment in time is a reflection of the sum total of all our thoughts and beliefs up to that moment in time. We are simultaneously living in the residual of our past, with unlimited potential based upon our current thoughts, beliefs and actions. There is no difference between what is going on in the moment, and what we have thought or are thinking.

Whatever emotions and actions we give the most thought and energy to we will manifest in our life. Whatever we put out into life through our thoughts, feelings and actions will come back to us by law.

The formula is simple:

- ❖ Thoughts create feelings.
- ❖ Feelings create vibrations.
- ❖ Vibrations create actions.
- ❖ Actions create results.

If we're going to use our mind and emotions for anything, let it be for thoughts and ideas that are creative and empowering. Living in fear or confusion will only bring destructive people and experiences into our lives. For me, one rock was enough!

Understanding the seven laws and the six faculties of the mind, and understanding the relationship between energy, vibration, thoughts and things, is the foundation for taking total responsibility for our lives. It's also the first step toward understanding how to live a full and abundant life...and how to restore peace on earth.

NINE

First Impressions

The love that I was when I was a child is the same love that I am today. Whether climbing mountains or resting quietly amidst the fallen leafs of autumn aspens, whether sharing my song or listening gently, whether seeking or finding or lost or found, the love that I have is the love that I AM…!
~ David Lloyd Strauss

MY TEN MINUTES PERCHED at the top of the crack canyon was a powerful time for me. It was interesting to see how quickly a simple image in nature reminded me of everything I had learned. That's how it is. Everything we're ever looking for is always very close…sometimes so close that we can't even see it.

It was now time to begin retracing my footsteps. The entire route is a rock-solid trail littered with small bits of stone, petroglyphs and a steady spotting of small cairns to mark the path. I paused often to reflect upon the beauty of the desert and to honor the flow of my emotions. My first full stop was along the Pueblo Alto loop at the New Alto Pueblo. I entered the pueblo with light footsteps and a humbled heart. I sat down on the edge of one of the crumbled walls, closed my eyes and reconnected with the feelings that had carried me off the plateau – feelings of hope and courage that had been driven by my fear of loss of life and my desire to live. As I stood between the walls, I had an incredible realization about the stories of our lives, our fears, walls, bridges and dreams. The walls of the ruins started speaking to me in pictures, and through these pictures I gained deeper insight into the journey of our lives.

If these walls could tell stories, I thought, I can only imagine what they would be. From the moment the Anasazi picked up the first stone to lay the foundation, to the spiritual ceremony that went on within this pueblo, I imagined the beating of drums...the scent of burning sage...the sound of instruments...the cooking, dancing and chanting. I imagined celebrations under the stars and ceremonies under the full moon. It must have been a magical lifestyle, living day-to-day, driven by deep spiritual beliefs rooted in a healthy respect for land and mother earth. As I imagined the singing voices, it occurred to me that it wasn't just the walls that had stories. We all have stories.

We are all storytellers. Each of us has our own story about who we are, what has happened to us, who or what did it to us, and how it affected us. Each of our lives is a unique story that reflects our conditioning as a child and the choices we have made since childhood. All our stories begin the same. We all start out as seeds and, through fertilization, grow into our genetic coding, which blends with the influences of our upbringing. The cycles of birth and death set the time boundaries of our lives, and what happens between those two points in time is our story. Our story can be a dream, a nightmare or an incredible tale of transformation, depending upon the beliefs we adhere to, the choices we make and the actions we take.

We are all dreamers. We all have dreams for our life. We have a dream lifestyle, a dream home, a dream vacation, a dream partner, a dream car, a dream wardrobe, a dream career, even a dream level of health and wellness. As children we had sandbox dreams. We would play in the sandbox and imagine ourselves as anything we wanted to be. We had no limits because we had no fear. Our hearts and minds were fresh and untainted, which made everything a possibility.

Childhood is the most magical time of our life because it represents our true nature. During childhood, our imagination is our entire world. We believe everything we can imagine. We even have imaginary friends and stuffed animals that talk with us and understand us. Our imagination is our story and our reality. It's the perfect life. We can have, do and be anything we want, simply by imagining. Everything is fantasy and reality at the same time. Everything is wonderful, delicious and exciting. We have endless potential to live, love and create.

> *The true sign of intelligence is not knowledge but imagination.*
> ~ *Albert Einstein*

Indulge your imagination for a moment and return to the time of your birth. Imagine that as soon as you were born, angels came into your life and gave you an invisible gift. They gave you a beautifully wrapped box with colorful wrapping paper, ribbons and bows. You're told that it is the gift of life and with it you can have, do and be anything you want. You are told that all the truth in the world, all the magic and power in the entire universe, is contained within the gift, and that you are to treasure, honor and respect it throughout your life. You are ever so excited because your very first experience out of the womb is a gift from angels. You love the bows and wrapping paper, and you feel ever so special to have received the gift of life. With the gentle trust, innocence and enthusiasm of a newborn, you begin to develop and grow, all the while doing your best to guard and hold onto your magical gift from the angels. But things begin to change. As time moves forward, you enter the most influential part of your growth. This is the time of first impressions. During this period you make the subtle transition from the innocence of a newborn child to being influenced by the outside world. Outside influences have a deep impact on the development of our consciousness in a manner similar to the birth of a duckling.

On any given spring day you can see a platoon of ducklings following their mother in a single file line. The ducklings follow their mother everywhere she goes. This urge to follow is a genetic behavior. When a duckling is born, the first creature it sees that is larger than itself imprints on the duckling's brain. From that moment forward, the duckling believe that it actually is that creature. For humans, our first impressions of life are based on the people who raise us and influence our thoughts and beliefs during our first five years. These first impressions have a deep and direct impact on how we will perceive life. Through these impressions, we slowly but unintentionally forget about the gift of life. Our entire system of thoughts and beliefs, including our behavior patterns, becomes shaped by what we experience and learn during this initial period of time. First impressions have a lasting impact because they bypass our conscious mind and embed directly into our subconscious mind.

Although most people identify themselves with their body, we are made up of far more than our physical body. Our experience of life is a reflection of our personality. And our personality is a blend of our physical body and our conscious and subconscious mind. Our entire sense of self-worth, how we perceive life, how we live each day, how we treat people, how we react or respond to circumstances, the experiences we attract, whether we are healthy or ill, are all shaped by our subconscious mind.

As babies, our subconscious mind is a blank slate, completely open to any ideas, thoughts and beliefs that are fed to us. Outside of any genetic predispositions, the first impressions we receive shape our entire pattern of beliefs and behavior. These patterns of belief are what determine our rules about life, love, failure, success, acceptance, rejection, confidence and fear. Environment is everything! Our overall sense of who we are, our habits and behaviors, our overall self-worth, is a reflection of whether we are raised by dream-weavers or dream-stealers.

Dream-weavers are the people who leave positive first impressions on our mind. Consciously or unconsciously, they understand the law of cause and effect, the relationship between thoughts, emotions and things. They understand that whatever we think and believe directly influences our experience of life. As a result, they fill our minds with love and encouragement, and they plant seeds of confidence and self-love by consistently focusing on what we are doing right, by encouraging us to become stronger and better. If we do something "wrong," they explain why it was wrong so that we can make better decisions in the future. They teach us how to build bridges and castles, not walls and moats. They teach us how to learn and grow through difficulties and challenges. They encourage us to use our imagination, and they participate in the stories we create in our minds. They teach us that there is no such thing as failure as long as we are learning from our actions. They tell us that everything is possible as long as we stay focused and consistent. If we fall down, they encourage us to get up and continue. They rarely say "no" or "don't." Instead, they speak to us with guidance, with a mentor's heart and mind, and teach us with interest and concern. They treat us like people, not like children. And through this mutual respect, we develop a healthy self-image. Kids that are raised by dream-weavers develop the personalities and attitudes of winners and achievers. They believe in possibilities. They see conflict as a challenge, and their self-confidence flourishes as they grow and mature. Their sense of self-worth is based on how they see themselves from the inside out, rather than on other people's opinions.

Dream-stealers leave negative first impressions on our mind. They do not understand the law of cause and effect, nor do they understand the relationship between thoughts, emotions and things. They raise their children through fear and negative influences. They do not do this intentionally. They just don't know any better. Dream-stealers are the ones who tell us we can't, warn us to be careful or, from a fearful place, say, "Don't do that. You may get hurt". They punish us more than they encourage us. And through their consistent negative counseling, we grow to become afraid of life. They put fear in our hearts and minds and make us question our imagination and our physical and creative abilities. Our natural potential becomes dwarfed by their fears, and our self-esteem flounders. We love them out of innocence because they are our parents, family or close friends. We trust them, so we want to believe them. But by believing them, we take on their energy and vibration. Their fears became ours. And our life takes on the same walls as theirs, walls built with stones of fear. Fear of failure. Fear of love. Fear of rejection. Fear of abandonment. There are unlimited fears, and unlimited stones and walls. Through these walls, we take on the dis-ease of being an adult, and our story changes from innocence to uncertainty. Fear replaces imagination, and our story takes on more and more chapters. We enter into the emotional conflict of having our dreams overpowered by our fears. We start to develop beliefs about why our dreams can't come true rather than why they can. For the remainder of our life we live safely within our walls.

Like most people, I was raised with plenty of love. But behind that love lurked a lot of dream-stealer thoughts and ideas that created deep negative seeds in my subconscious mind — seeds of fear of failure and fear of poverty, lack and limitation. I had the same experiences that most kids had. I was told that children should be seen and not heard. As a result, I grew up being afraid to speak the thoughts that were in my heart and mind. I was told that if I didn't get good grades, I wouldn't be able to get ahead in life. Yet at the same time, I was continually shown what I did wrong. If I got three questions wrong on an exam, I was given a red "-3," not a "+97." I became afraid of failure because our education system focuses on mistakes rather than successes. Our report cards influence our self-esteem because we are told that the A and B students are the ones who will be successful. As a result, we strive for a letter instead of working to build our intelligence. Little do we realize as kids that the A and B students are very often the ones who will end up working for companies owned and by the C and D students. When I was daydreaming in class, using my imagination to envision my dreams, I was scolded and told to pay attention. Thus I associated using my imagination with fear and was conditioned to memorize information rather than flourish with creativity. I was told that I had to be like others in order to be loved and accepted. So I learned how to act the way I thought other people perceived me, rather than learning how to love and be myself. I learned how to live from the outside in because I was told that, overall, I had to conform to a set of rules and outside expectations in order to be loved and accepted. I spent most of my childhood in a struggle between wanting to be myself and, at the same time, wanting to be accepted by others.

Like everyone, I want my dreams to come true. I want to succeed in life. But our culture does not reward success. It rewards pain, mediocrity and failure. Our culture resents people who prosper financially. When someone does well, the rest of the world wants a handout. Yet we get plenty of love and support when we go through difficult times. We are conditioned to be victims. We learn to make excuses to justify our fears and failures. We learn to be helpless because there is plenty of love and support when there is pain.

Most of the world is raised by dream-stealers. That means that most of the world has had negative images placed into their conscious and subconscious mind. As a result, most of humanity lives in fear, poverty, lack and limitation. And most of the world develops the perception that our life is something that happens to us from the outside in rather than something we create from the inside out. Self-worth becomes based upon the approval and validation of others, rather than on our own image of ourselves. To protect ourselves from our fear of failure or rejection, we mask ourselves from our true identity and trade our unlimited potential for learned helplessness and victim consciousness. We become too afraid to take responsibility for our own lives and blame others for the "bad" things that happen to us. We want the world to change so that we don't have to. We believe that as long as we are "victims," people will feel sorry for us and show us love out of pity or sorrow.

Our life is our very own personal screenplay. We are the writer, the actor, the stage and the director of our entire experience of life. Whether we are children of dream-weavers or dream-stealers, the degree to which we own our personal power or yield it to others is a reflection of our self-image. The way we see ourselves is the paintbrush that determines how alive and full of life we truly are. No matter where we are on the scale of self-worth, the strength of our personal power and self-image impacts every area of our life. Our entire experience of life is based on our self-image because our self-image defines the people we associate with, the choices we make and the actions we take. Our self-image determines our health, our wealth, our happiness and, ultimately, the story we believe and share about ourselves.

The story that we believe and share with others about our life is not the truth. It is only our story. And our story is a direct reflection of the meaning we have chosen to give to the events of our life. People with a healthy level of self-worth have an empowering story and go into situations seeing and feeling their success in advance. People with low self-worth have a disempowering story. They are afraid of success because they are simultaneously afraid of failure.

As we go through our day-to-day lives, we are constantly making choices based upon the habitual thoughts and beliefs of our story. Many of our choices are conscious and intentional. But most are rooted in the core beliefs stored in our subconscious mind and are reflected as our ongoing mental and emotional habits and conditioning. These choices are what create our story. Our story is self-fulfilling and will carry on throughout our lives, because our story is based on our thoughts and beliefs, each of which carries its own unique frequency. Our story is a magnetic force based on the law of vibration that will attract into our lives people, places and circumstances that are in harmony with our core thoughts, beliefs and emotions.

We all know that we are capable of so much more. Yet we are addicted to our story because it is familiar and because we are unaware that we are stuck in it at a subconscious, energetic and vibrational level. We end up in a loop. Our life becomes our story and our story creates our life. Very few people realize that the meaning we give to our experiences is what creates our story and that our story is what shapes our life. Even fewer realize that we have complete control over the direction of our life because we choose what our experiences mean to us. The law of relativity gives us power over our story and our circumstances because we always have the choice to change our beliefs and change our perception.

If we were raised by dream-stealers, it is our choice and challenge to unglue the grips of a negative system of thoughts and beliefs, reclaim our personal power and enter into the journey of developing a healthy sense of self-worth. For all of us, regardless of how we see ourselves, our life can only grow and expand as much as our story allows us to. Nothing in life will ever change as long as we continue to believe and tell the same story. Within our story lies what we believe to be possible or impossible. We can never move in a direction that our mind believes to be impossible.

All that we are is the result of what we have thought. The mind is everything. What we think we become.
~ Buddha

One of the most valuable skills we can learn is pattern recognition. When the time comes, as it often does, that we want to change the direction of our life, the first step is to become clear about the patterns in our life that are showing up as our story. Once we are aware of this, the next step is to use the power of our thoughts and imagination to craft a new story. When we redefine the meanings we have given to the experiences of our past, when we change our perceptions of life, we change our story. We liberate ourselves from the ball-and-chain of our past and create a new canvas for our dreams to manifest upon. Unfortunately, few people will ever change their story. Instead, not knowing that their lives are a reflection of their story, most will go through their lives thinking that there is something wrong with them, rather than understanding that it's their story, their core subconscious beliefs about themselves and life, that is creating their experiences.

I am here right now because a rock gave me a sudden and unexpected opportunity to change my story. I changed my story from believing that there was something wrong with me that needed to be fixed to believing that I am a hero. I believe that I am a hero because the cards were stacked against me since my childhood. With all the difficulties in my life and all the mistakes I have made, there were many times where I could have pushed the self-destruct button. Instead, I chose life. When people were putting me down, I held tight and lifted myself up. I'm a hero because I'm still alive, still willing to learn, grow, forgive and forget. I'm a hero because I still believe in my dreams, I still believe in love and I still believe in humanity. I'm a hero because I believe in possibilities. I believe it is possible for humanity to wake up from our ignorant slumber, to start taking responsibility for the conditions of our world and to start taking action toward change. I believe that every adversity in life is a seed that offers us an opportunity to learn something new, to grow stronger and wiser, to be our own hero, and to be the hero for our largest self – the self of all of creation.

At the core of my story and everyone's story, at the core of transmuting our negative story into an empowering story, are the inescapable laws of energy. Our story is based on our thoughts and beliefs about life. Thoughts are things. Beliefs are thoughts. Whatever beliefs we consistently give power and emotion to will continuously manifest in our lives. The first impressions in our life were the thoughts that shaped our self-image and set the vibrational tone of our journey through life. The life we are living and all the experiences we are having, whether we like them or not, are occurring by law. The patterns of experiences that we call habits or chronic problems will continue to show up until we take massive action to improve our self-image, change our story and adopt a new, more empowering set of beliefs into our subconscious mind.

Everyone has experienced their version of my falling rock. Problems are a sign of life. If we did not have them, we would not grow. Every problem or challenge is a response to a past action or decision. Our decisions and actions affect every aspect of our lives. We attract rocks because we create them. We draw into our lives the experiences that are in harmony with our thoughts, emotions and subconscious beliefs. It doesn't matter what hits us on the head. Each and every one of us, at some point in our lives has had a difficult experience and has had the choice to either take total responsibility for the event or blame our "rock" for our problem. When we blame, it is because we have subconsciously developed the habit of being a victim and have given our personal power away to people, places or circumstances. A rock can be any painful experience. It can be childhood abuse or death of a loved one. It can be a family member, a friend, a boss, a lost lover, a teacher, a politician, the government, an injury or disease, drugs, alcohol, food or financial setbacks. It can be anyone and anything.

Our rock is whatever we want it to be. It can be the springboard that brings change into our life or the object of our blame. We can become addicted to the pain it brings or we can become empowered by the inner strength we gain. Regardless of the choice we make, we are individually responsible for the walls we build, and we are the only ones who can tear them down and build bridges in their place. If we don't choose to work on tearing down our walls, life will bring us experiences that will force our walls down. And those experiences will be a lot more painful than if we do it voluntarily.

My rock was an "involuntary" intervention in my life. I was a master mason at wall-building. I built castles with my fears and locked myself in the dungeons below. They were beautiful castles, and I thought they would protect me forever. I was wrong. My rock knocked a hole in my walls and woke me up. It woke me up to the truth that all our dreams are on the other side of our walls and that the only way to tear down those walls is to change our story. The way to change our story is to become teachable, to ask different questions about life and circumstances and to be willing to change the meaning we have given to our experiences. We have to take an inventory of the experiences we have associated pain with and create a new, empowering question and a new, empowering meaning. We have to look for the opportunity in the adversity. If we can't find it, we must create it. By doing this, we change our vibration and begin to attract new people and experiences into our lives.

When we change our story our walls tumble to the ground. We can then begin to use the same stones to create bridges towards our dreams — bridges of love, gratitude, abundance, caring, generosity, acceptance, creativity and compassion.

All roads lead to love and light. All side roads and diversions lead to experience, growth, wisdom and understanding. We will all make it through the maze. It is just a matter of how, when and under what conditions. The four keys for moving through that gateway are responsibility, forgiveness and gratitude.

TEN

Responsibility and Forgiveness

If you must speak ill of another, do not speak it, write it in the sand near the water's edge.
~Napoleon Hill

RECOGNIZING THAT WE HAVE the power to turn our walls into bridges can be an invaluable tool for transforming any difficulty into a source of inspiration and strength. On the other side of all challenges, for those with the courage to look beyond the appearances of the current conditions of their life, there is always an opportunity for personal growth, rebirth and rejuvenation.

After leaving the walls of the New Alto Pueblo, I continued along the Pueblo Alto Loop trail, feeling, with every step, like a ghost on the trail of its past. The last time I had walked here, I had been covered in my own blood on a mission of self-rescue. It all seemed like a dream to me now. Everything looked familiar. Yet that dramatic episode seemed unreal.

This whole journey of retracing my footsteps after the fall was like looking in a double mirror. I was reflecting upon the reflections of my past. I was here this day because the emotional impact of this experience had caused me to take a nosedive into the hall of mirrors and look closely at all my thoughts, beliefs and intentions. I was here because I knew that the lessons of this experience were invaluable, and had to be shared.

While I was looking into that mirror, it had become very clear to me that this was no accident. I had attracted that rock to my head with the same force as metal to a magnet. I had attracted it because the story that was then going on in my mind about my life had been ready to end and transform and it had taken the disruptive force of a rock to get my attention and bring about the change. Being forced into a position to be honest with myself about my story and my thoughts and beliefs was a giant leap in my path of self-awareness.

Even though I didn't die physically that day, when that rock hit me on the head, I truly believed that my life was ending. When I woke up, I was completely surprised to still be alive. That contrast gave me the priceless emotional experience of death. At the core of my experience is the lesson of total self-responsibility and the surrendering of blame, guilt and resentment, along with any idea of being a victim.

It is easy to blame people and circumstances for our problems and challenges and to look outwardly for reasons to justify our pain. Yet when faced with adversity, those who understand the laws of life take the time to look within and to seek from within the flaws in their own character. They look within because they have learned that life is an inner journey and that the people, circumstance and experiences they will attract into their lives will depend upon where they are on that journey.

Blame never helped anyone resolve anything. It certainly wouldn't have helped me had I blamed the rock for hitting me. Blame doesn't fix anything. As long as we blame, as long as we act like a victim, we resist the laws and give our power away. However, giving our power away does not change the laws. Blame does nothing more than deny us the ability to make changes in our life. Taking total responsibility for our life — for our thoughts, decisions, actions and experiences — is the only thing that can save us from the rocks in our life.

We all make mistakes. We all make choices that bring pain to ourselves or others. Once we get past the pain, though, we must remember that all experiences occur by law. Once we are at the age where we can think for ourselves, we can no longer be the victim of someone else's doing without taking some degree of responsibility for having co-created the experience through our thoughts, feelings and actions. We are responsible for what we think, feel and do. No one else can make us think, feel or act in any particular way. No one can make us feel happy or sad, ugly or attractive, loved or unloved. Our feelings and actions are always a reflection of our thoughts and beliefs about our self and life. We may not like all the experiences that show up. We may try and blame other people or circumstances for how we feel. We may try to deny responsibility for our lives. But, ultimately, the emotions we feel, the actions we take and the mistakes we make are our own doing. They are a reflection of our beliefs and our self-image. Our difficulties can be the doorways to our greatest lessons. And our so-called enemies can be our greatest teachers in disguise.

Accept responsibility for your life. Know that it is you who will get you where you want to go, no one else. If you fall, fall on your back. If you can look up, you can get up.
~ *Les Brown*

Few people are raised to take responsibility for their lives. Most of us are raised to blame people and circumstances. Do not be like most people. Don't be a victim of your own choices or your own ambivalence. If you are not happy with the direction of your life — if you are in a dead-end job or a tired or abusive relationship — if you are unhealthy — if you lack self-respect, or are just not satisfied — then quit observing your dissatisfaction. Quit wallowing in the pain. Quit feeling sorry for yourself. Quit staring at your rock. Do something about it. Take action! Be the cause of the change in your own life! You are fully capable of taking total responsibility for your own life. It starts with the decision to do so.

In order to bring change into your life, you have to make room for the change. You have to let go of something. Let go of that which no longer serves your highest good. Let go of the people, places, circumstances and habits that are causing you to hold yourself back. This includes letting go of disempowering and self-limiting thoughts and beliefs. Let go. Don't look back. If you want to be happy, it's your responsibility. If you want to be healthy, it's your responsibility. If you want to be wealthy, it's your responsibility. If you want to reinvent your life, it's your responsibility. Be the voice and master of your destiny. Make a decision to set your sights forward, to take action and to take total responsibility for everything that happens in your life. Period! Don't worry about what other people think about your choices. It's your life. You have to live with yourself. The only thing that matters is what you think and feel about yourself.

Let go of your fears. Let go of your grudges. Release yourself from the shackles and chains of pointing blame. Take complete responsibility for your life and circumstances. Take responsibility by setting a new standard and taking action. Draw a line in the sand, walk away from your past and step into your dreams. Take responsibility for your attitude, thoughts, beliefs and emotions. Take responsibility for your choices and actions. Most importantly, take responsibility for the meaning you give to each and every one of your experiences. If you don't know how to achieve the new outcome for your life, find a mentor. Find someone who has the results that you want, follow in their footsteps and learn from them.

We all go through life working through our choices and challenges and being confronted with our lessons. No matter how painful things are at the moment, embrace the opportunity to learn and grow. Within every experience is the seed and opportunity for greatness. Do not stand in judgment of what anyone has done to you, or what you have done to yourself. Reclaim your personal power, and surrender all blame. You are not a victim of anyone or anything unless you choose to be. The hero you are looking for to rescue you is YOU!

This lesson of total self-responsibility is in deep contrast to the victim-consciousness that has hijacked the hearts of humanity. Regardless of the events in our lives, until we surrender our self-indulged story and take full responsibility for the situations we find ourselves in, we can never move forward. We alone are responsible for the outcome of the events in our lives because we choose the actions we take and the meaning we give to our experiences.

How much of your past do you really want to hold onto? How much of your pain do you want to keep in your life? Are you willing to trade the grip on your past for the gift of your freedom and peace of mind? You can't have both. You cannot have one foot in the past while trying to move forward. You cannot drive ahead if you're always looking in the rearview mirror. People who move forward in life know how to let go, take action and take total responsibility for their lives. They know how to make quick decisions and keep those decisions. If the circumstance they desire do not yet exist, they create the circumstances. They do not wait for things to happen. They make things happen. Responsibility is the sail and the wind to our freedom and to our dreams.

If you don't understand or know why something happened, treat it as if you did. Take total responsibility. Everything that is happening is occurring by law. When we grow to understand and trust these laws, we don't need to see or understand the entire string of events that brought the experience into our lives. We just have to know that the laws of life work in our favor as long as we work with them, not against them.

The most effective way to take total responsibility for our lives and reclaim our personal power is by letting go of the four emotional black holes of anger, resentment, guilt and blame. Whenever we feel a negative emotion toward another person we are only harming ourselves because we are the ones who are feeling the negative emotion, not them. Someone may do something painful to us once, but we do it to ourselves thousands of times by reliving the memory of the experience. Continuously reflecting upon a painful experience is like watching a bad movie over and over again. You wouldn't waste your time or emotions repeatedly watching a bad movie. So why keep the memory of pain alive? There is a one-step process to letting go. It's called forgiveness.

Forgiveness is the ultimate recipe for freedom. Forgiveness is the tool and toolbox for transformation. It is the saw that cuts off the chains that shackle us to our past. It is the eternal elixir that cures the idle heart from the ills of past pain and makes room for a return to love. A forgiving person is someone who knows how to tend to the garden of the mind. Anger, resentment, guilt and blame are weeds that strangle our thoughts and blind our heart. Forgiving is simply letting go of our idea of what we think happened, taking responsibility for our lives and pulling the weeds of hateful thoughts from the garden of our mind. It's not easy to pull weeds, it's not easy to take responsibility and forgive. But it's worth it.

Here's what A Course in Miracles says about forgiveness:

Forgiveness offers everything I want. What could you want forgiveness cannot give? Do you want peace? Forgiveness offers it. Do you want happiness, a quiet mind, a certainty of purpose, and a sense of worth and beauty that transcends the world? Do you want care and safety, and the warmth of sure protection always? Do you want a quietness that cannot be disturbed, a gentleness that never can be hurt, a deep, abiding comfort, and a rest so perfect it can never be upset?

All this forgiveness offers you, and more. It sparkles on your eyes as you awake, and gives you joy with which to meet the day. It soothes your forehead while you sleep, and rests upon your eyelids so you see no dreams of fear and evil, malice and attack. And when you wake again, it offers you another day of happiness and peace. All this forgiveness offers you, and more. (A Course In Miracles – 122)

Forgiveness can be more than just letting go. There is a higher level of forgiveness that is for the bravest of hearts. If to forgive is to let go, then the only reason we would ever need to forgive is if we blamed someone for something. There is no blame where there is total self-responsibility. The only person we ever need to forgive is ourselves. When we surrender blame, when we finally take total responsibility for our life and no longer blame anyone for anything, we step away from the emotional roller coaster of blame and forgiveness and move to the highest level of self-empowerment. At this level, when we say, "I forgive you," we are really saying, "I don't blame you. Thank you for being a mirror of my thoughts and beliefs and for having given me the opportunity to look at my own role in what just occurred."

A belief in total self-responsibility does not deny painful experiences. It's about realizing that the experiences of life are neutral and have no meaning. The law of relativity gives us the freedom to decide whether things are "good" or "bad." We decide to either learn and grow or shrivel up and die. We decide what to do with our experiences. We can grow stronger or weaker, more rigid or more flexible. We can gain more personal power or give more power away.

When I made the choice to rescue myself, what I really did was reclaim my personal power. I didn't have to forgive (blame) the rock for hitting me. I had to forgive myself for the choices I had made in life that had pushed this intervention into my life.

That rock may have taken some of my blood and scalp, but it gave me back my personal power. I have since made the choice that the circumstances of my life will not dictate the direction of my life. I have declared: I am the voice and master of my destiny!

ELEVEN

The Power of Colors

The storms of life are the pathway to healing, and the gusts of change are the mother of creation. It is light that gives life, and it is life that gives light.
~ David Lloyd Strauss

WHILE HIKING ALONG, thinking about the path of total self-responsibility, the last thing I wanted was a repeat of my previous experience. I paused for a moment and realized that the weather on this day was similar to the day of my injury: hot and dry, with a light dusting of clouds. Desert heat is something to be cautious about, so I slowed my footsteps and took a break to cool off under a shaded rock overhang.

As I looked out over the desert terrain, I thought about the depth to which the laws of nature interact with each other and how they work together to shape everything in life. It was all so obvious, yet entirely hidden.

I saw the full symphony of all the laws of energy dancing together in a divinely orchestrated symposium of love and creativity. I saw an incredible bouquet of vibrations wearing the garment and costume of colors, textures, scent, density and aliveness. It was the bouquet of bouquets. The pièce de resistance of nature's creation. I was standing amidst the mirrors of life.

Everywhere I turned, I saw the stroke of creation painted as the canvas of mother earth. Everything blended to create a mystical image of life. The picture I saw was a picture of infinite possibilities. The picture I felt with my heart and emotions was the silent joy of the ebb and flow of life's tide of changes.

I closed my eyes, entered into a place of peaceful meditation and retreated into the world within as I listened to the sound of the desert. It was the sound of silence with a light dusting of soft wind gently caressing my thoughts and imagination. I slowed my breath, listened to the beating of my heart and imagined it to be the beating of Anasazi drums during a celebration of the sun. Palms touching palms, fingers touching fingers, I placed my hands in front of my heart. Then I raised my head directly toward the sun and allowed its energy to pass through my eyelids and into my pupils. With the cadence of my breath matching the beating of my heart, I imagined the light flowing through my eyes and into the center of my head, then gently washing through my body with the grace of a flowing river. The light then passed through my head, down my neck and into my shoulders, elbows, wrists and fingers. From my fingers, it flowed into the air with the grace of a gentle stream. Then, the light passed through my heart and lungs, through every organ in my body, and down through my hips, knees, ankles, feet and toes...and back into the earth. For a single moment, I imagined myself to be as still as a tree, with my only movement matching the gentle push of the wind. My feet felt like roots deeply embedded in the heart and soul of mother earth. What a beautiful experience, reaching out to the sun while the sun reached into me. As the sun poured through my eyelids, into my eyes and scattered throughout my body, it refracted into the seven colors of the rainbow, and I felt the power of each color.

I felt the vigor of Red, the color of energy, strength, passion, motivation, adventure, survival and security.

I danced with the bliss of Orange, an uplifting, stimulating color of joy, excitement, movement, creativity, sexuality, spontaneity, fun and pleasure.

I was revitalized with the brightness of Yellow, a refreshing color that enlivens personal power, lightness of heart, self-control, clarity and focus.

I was reassured with the soothing color of Green, the color of earth, offering comfort and protection, emanating balance, harmony, healing, stability, compassion, love and kindness.

I bathed in the tranquil feeling of Blue, the color of a crystal-like energy that is calming, protective, cooling and soothing.

I felt the calmness of Violet, the color of introspection, confidence, intuition, self-respect and dignity...the color of meditation and inner reflection.

With my heart, mind and body flowing with the colors of sunshine, I imagined my entire body healed. I imagined each beam of color dancing through the residue of my injuries and reshaping my body by kneading my muscles, tendons, bones and brain cells with the energy and power of light. If light can grow a tree, a flower, a cactus or juniper, I thought, if light can melt ice and illuminate the earth and skies, it can certainly empower the healing of my own body.

It was in that moment that I understood the words of Hawkwind: "We cannot heal our body, until we first heal our mind."

I saw and felt the lesson of sunshine. Energy flows where attention goes. In this beautiful moment, I was giving my attention to the sun and the wind and, through this, energy flowed into and throughout my body, scattering my thoughts of lack and limitation. It now became clear: Negative thoughts are like glue and tar to the flow of energy, speed bumps to emotional and physical healing. Light and love are the ultimate solvent but can only be released with an open, forgiving heart and mind. We cannot have faith and doubt at the same time. We cannot desire healing and focus on negative thoughts and dis-ease. We cannot want light and love in our life while focusing on darkness. Our perception of the moment is what shapes the moment. Our perception of healing is what shapes the healing.

I opened my eyes and gave deeper thought to the journey of healing. In the same way that emotions are a feedback mechanism to show us what we are thinking, our body also gives us feedback, but on a deeper level. If we have a chronic, negative or self-destructive way of thinking, if we have unhealthy eating habits, if we smoke, if we lack physical exercise, it shows up as injury or disease in the moment when our body can no longer handle the abuse. While the body does have some ability to heal itself, it too has limits. Injury and disease are a symptom of when we have reached that limit. They are an effect rather than a cause. If we don't change our thoughts, habits and behavior, the body will continue to give us feedback through new or recurring injuries, or chronic pain or disease.

If you drove on a road covered with nails every day, would you complain about flat tires? Of course not. Flat tires are feedback that you're on a bad road. Likewise, illness, disease, and injury are feedback that you're on the wrong road. You change roads by changing your thoughts feelings, actions and lifestyle.

Most medications deal with symptom relief. Symptoms are feedback from our body that something is out of alignment. If we address the symptom, it does not eliminate the cause. If we continuously medicate or ignore symptoms, the dis-ease becomes chronic. Doctors can provide the wonderful service of diagnosis and offer a lot of tools to guide the healing of the body. But they can't fix our thoughts and beliefs. They can't change our eating habits or lifestyle, all of which, ultimately, have the largest impact on our overall health and wellness. Only we can do that.

Our bodies are a mass of molecules in a very high speed of vibration. They are made up of the same energy and intelligence that all thoughts and things are made of. Every cell and organ of the human body is its own reservoir of energy and has its own unique frequency of vibration within which it can exist in a healthy state. The energy emanating from the human body, often referred to as an "aura," is measurable through Kirlian photography, which was first discovered in 1939 by Semyon Kirlian.

Outside of any genetic predisposition for disease, if our thoughts, feelings, eating patterns and fitness habits violate the harmonic vibration of our body, injury and disease are very likely to show up. What we eat and think has a direct, energetic impact on the overall health of our body, and our bodies ability to heal itself. The food we eat either gives us energy or takes it away, depending on the quality and energetic vibration of the food. On the level of thought, it is becoming more widely accepted in Western medicine that the energy of our thoughts has a dramatic, if not a direct impact on our physical health — so much so that it has become clear that even a chronic fear of injury or disease can actually manifest the symptom of the disease or bring about experiences that will cause the injury. When we are prone to injuries, it has more to do with where our minds are, rather than what we are doing.

There are several steps to the healing of the mind and changing our patterns of thinking. First and foremost, we have to understand that our thoughts and behaviors, and any chronic ways of thinking, are an out-picturing of the beliefs stored in our subconscious mind. These thoughts and beliefs are like a song we can't get out of our mind. The best way to stop the song is to scratch the CD so that it can never play again. Healing the mind is the equivalent of scratching a CD. When the scratch is deep enough, it can't be played any more. The same is true with our thoughts and beliefs. We can't undo or remove our thoughts and behavior patterns from our subconscious mind. However, we can interrupt the pattern of thinking and add new, empowering thoughts and ideas, which, through consistency of action and attention, will override our old thoughts and bring to form our new system of beliefs.

At the core of healing the mind is the understanding of the relationship between energy, thoughts, emotions and things. With this understanding, the first step is to pay close attention to our thoughts, and to any chronic, negative, self-limiting or self-destructive thought patterns. If we are not sure of what our negative thoughts are, the best place to look is the results that have shown up in our life, including our recurring challenges, because they are a reflection of our thoughts. In addition, any words that we put after the words "I AM" when we describe ourselves clearly indicate our negative, self-destructive and self-limiting thoughts. Once we identify our thoughts, we can use the law of polarity to put into writing words opposite to those negative thoughts, words that are positive, empowering expressions of gratitude for the new identity and outcome. Using our imagination with vivid accuracy and detail, we can internalize these new thoughts and create positive, happy, grateful, energizing images and feelings associated with these new thoughts. Next, we can start taking action by making changes that empower and reinforce these new thoughts and feelings.

Changing our thoughts and beliefs is not spontaneous. The law of gender makes it clear that everything has an incubation period. We must treat these new thoughts, along with the new outcome we hold for our life, with the same care as we would with take with a Chinese bamboo. We must begin to catch ourselves in our old thought patterns. As soon as we notice that old pattern, we must immediately affirm the empowering beliefs until we develop a new, consistent system of thinking, feeling and believing, and this new system shows up as results in our life.

The most difficult work we will ever do is to examine our own thoughts and beliefs, replace them with new ones, and hold those new thoughts and beliefs consistently in our mind and reinforce them through action. The subconscious thoughts and beliefs that we have accumulated since childhood do not want to let go their grip on our mind. It takes a sincere and deep wanting-to-change to tap into the strength necessary to break this grip. With consistency of thought and action, powered by vivid images and feelings, it can be done, and the outcome is worth every step of the journey.

If you are under medical care when you are looking to integrate the science of thoughts and feelings into physical healing of injury or disease, follow your doctor's guidance while at the same time listening to your intuition and exploring the many possibilities of working on your own thoughts and beliefs. There are times when the tools of western medicine are highly appropriate. However, there are plenty of stories of people who have integrated western medicine with self-healing or healed their bodies entirely through understanding the impact of thoughts, proper nutrition and exercise. This is entirely a personal choice. I certainly would prefer self-healing, when appropriate, over invasive surgery or medicine.

Looking through the lens of my dance with the rock, the healing of my body was far quicker than the healing of my mind. I had a lot of self-destructive thoughts and patterns that were abruptly interrupted through my hernia and concussion. It took quite some time to open my heart and mind to be totally honest with myself about my overall thoughts and beliefs. The gift of this experience is that I now understand the natural flow to energy and, therefore, the natural flow to healing.

We choose our thoughts. Our thoughts create our feelings. Our feelings determine our vibration and actions, and our actions shape our results. Our mind is what determines what is going on in both our outside world and the inner world of the condition of our body. Healing starts with a thought, an image in our conscious mind that then flows into our subconscious mind. The subconscious mind will accept anything that the conscious mind accepts. The images we accept control the vibration of our body, which directly affects the healing of our body.

We are totally responsible for the healing of our mind and the results in our life. It comes down to understanding the impact of our thoughts, feelings and actions, and to being consciously aware of what we think and feel.

Standing at the desert overlook, I realized that I did have a choice when it came to my own health and wellbeing. At that thought, my face became electrified with joy and my body beamed with happiness. I raised my hands toward the sky and I said yes to life.

I am so happy and grateful now that I am healed!

TWELVE

The Collage of Life

You are an expression of this vast and wondrous universe. You are one of the things the universe is doing right now. This immense, mysterious existence is expressing itself everywhere at every moment. For the miracle to be expressed through you, it will take courage and a firm dedication to truth and honesty.
~ *Ralph Waldo Emerson*

STILL STANDING BY the cliff overhang, beaming with a refreshed perception of life, I cast my eyes upon the desert landscape and saw the world with the innocence of a child.

Life is as diverse as our eyes will see and our imagination will allow. There is no end to the variety of life. From every ray of sunshine to every cloud in the sky, from every tree and plant to every speck of dust upon the ground, the universe is a collage of energetic diversity.

Each person, animal, planet, moon, sun, star, flower, tree, plant and critter is a unique expression all its own. Everything is different. Nothing is the same. Nothing! This world of limitless potential is the garden in the mind of God and a manifestation of the laws of energy. Life is a bountiful salad of energetic vibrations. There are infinite possibilities for how energy can shape and express itself. Everything is a part of the whole. There is no separation but there is polarity and rhythm and relationships and change. Everything exists in terms of its opposite. Everything has a pulse and a rhythm. Everything has a cause and effect. Everything grows and evolves in its own time. Everything is growing and transmuting into something else. Everything is relative to everything else. These laws of energy create the collage of life and unite all of life. The differences are superficial. Beyond surface appearances and physical limitations, we are still one.

The entire experience of life is a charade. Life is playing hide-and-go-seek with itself. We are here not to blend in and fit in and be like everyone else. We are here to discover, express and enjoy our unique gifts, talents and abilities. Our uniqueness is what gives beauty to the bouquet of life. Our sameness is what keeps the matrix together. This bouquet of life, the world we live in, is a dance of infinite possibilities for experience and expression.

Our planet is a beautiful landscape of differences. There is no joy in trying to be like others. There is no real love when we try to change ourselves in order fit in and be accepted by others. All the joy in the world is found in discovering and celebrating our uniqueness and individuality. If everything were the same or were trying to be the same, there would be no beauty to the desert, the mountains, the oceans, the rivers or the streams. How could a flower garden, vegetable garden, fruit salad or vegetable salad be beautiful, aromatic or deliciously yummy if everything were the same? The creative energy behind the matrix of life has made everything different. Our universe is built upon differences. Life is a dance, a collage, a tapestry, a bouquet of diversity. We are each unique and different by design, not by accident.

We each have hidden talents — unique and special gifts to give to this world. We are diamonds in the rough. If we honor and celebrate our individuality, time will polish and brighten us. The greatest gift we can give to the world is to be ourselves. We are all unique and beautiful, each in our own way. By shining from the very center of our being, we can illuminate the world with the gift of our individuality.

We are each a flower in the garden of the mind of God. We need not try to do anything but be ourselves. We need not search out beauty or love elsewhere, only within ourselves. The tulip, the rose and the daisy do not fight for their identity. Put them together and you have a bouquet no less brilliant or colorful than the images in our hearts and minds. Can a bouquet have too many flowers or a rose too many petals? The power of one flower creates the beauty of the garden and the awesomeness of a garden is created through the efforts of many. The beauty of the bouquet comes from the scent and color of the family of flowers. The beauty of humanity comes from the family of individuals.

Life is about being, not doing. We are human beings, not human "doings." We can express our being-ness in any fashion we choose. Be it as a singer, dancer, traveler, student, artist, engineer or any manner of self-identification, we express our inner being through the joy of variety. There is nothing but diversity in life. To celebrate diversity is to celebrate our most beautiful quality. We are here to discover and celebrate all that we are and all that we can be, as individuals and collectively as humanity.

When you dance, your purpose is not to get to a certain place on the floor. It's to enjoy each step along the way.
~ Wayne Dyer

Our unique self-expression, the dance we bring to life, is our gift to the world. However varied and unique, we are each as beautiful and valuable as a flake of snow on a winter plateau. Our uniqueness is a natural part of the collage of life. There is only one self, one heart, one mind. That self is infinitely and collectively expressed as every person, animal, tree, rock and flower...as every individualized animate and inanimate object in this infinite universe.

The journey of life is different for everyone. We are all here to learn, grow, evolve and expand. We all have different levels of awareness and understanding. We are each born into different families, different cultures and different periods of time. Every individual who was ever born has had an unique experience and perspective on life. All individuals have their own strengths and weaknesses, their own thoughts and beliefs about life. There is no way around it. We are each unique expressions of infinite possibility, with unlimited potential to do, be and have whatever we want.

We are given the most incredible opportunity imaginable: to be a part of and enjoy the most beautiful experience in life, the experience of our own magic and beauty, the experience of our own authentic self. More than that, we are given the opportunity to dance the most magnificent dance ever orchestrated: the dance of life, the dance of difference, the dance of abundance. We are given the opportunity to embrace all the differences within nature and humanity, to honor individuality and to discover our own dance, which then adds to the bouquet of the true nature of life.

This bouquet of life, this collage of differences, is an incredible dance of harmony. Nature lives in harmony with itself. Everything allows everything to be. The sun does not judge the moon for interfering with its light. They work together to share the light abundantly and to regulate the flow of the tides. The earth does not judge the stars. They are both different, yet each gives the other space in the vastness of the universe. The birds do not judge each other. Each is different, yet all share the same wind and skies. The waters do not judge the land. They work together to distribute their goodness to all of life. All the differences in life are designed to work together in a spirit of cooperation.

Our differences give us strength. The laws of nature are here to protect and care for us, not to condemn and enslave us. What we see in nature is a blessing to humanity, when we open our hearts and minds to see the example it offers.

We are here not to learn, but to remember...to remember that all our differences only mask the fabric that connects us all. Our differences bring a unique perspective to life. Our individuality is our gift to the world. There is true power in living from the heart, in being true to our unique nature.

People notice people who live from the heart and are true to their core sense of self.

By being authentic and by expressing the individuality of your heart, you let the natural light of who you are shine forth. People will then be drawn to the light that shines from within you. They will ask how and why you are so happy, beautiful and at peace. Your answer is simple: "I took a journey into the collage of life, and therein I found everything I was seeking."

Celebrate your individuality!

THIRTEEN

Fear – Struggle – Courage

There is no greater gift to yourself and to those around you than your deciding to dump struggle, for struggle is an unholy battle that you fight with yourself. To go beyond struggle, you have to go beyond rigid opinion. That means opening yourself up to change.
~ *Stuart Wilde*

MY TWENTY MINUTES at the shaded rock overhang was a beautiful look into the mirror of life. But now it was time to continue on toward my destination: to the rock that set me free. I gathered my gear and returned to the trail. As I moved forward, it occurred to me that all the beauty and diversity I saw around me did not come without fear or struggle. Everything in life involves some sort of struggle. Nothing occurs instantly. The seed must struggle to take root and grow. Wild animals must struggle to find their next feed. The caterpillar does not instantly transform into a butterfly but must go through a very specific gestation period before it can transform. Its greatest strength comes when it is breaking out of its cocoon. The struggle to break free is what strengthens its wings. Caterpillars do not transform because they want to. They do so because it is their nature to accept and embrace change, just as it is ours.

Everything changes. It is the law of transmutation of energy. My injury and self-rescue, and my entire period of physical and emotional recovery, was a time of great fear and struggle. But it was also a time when I embraced change, strengthened my wings and tapped into a deep reservoir of inner courage, healing and understanding.

It is in our times of deepest need that we discover the depth of our courage...or the strength of our fear. Whatever our journey in life, each step forward brings us to a different place in time, to a unique experience. We all have moments where everything seems to fall apart. It could be a financial setback, ill health, death of a loved one, a collapsed relationship or a physical, mental or emotional breakdown. Whatever it is, harnessing the strength to work through these difficulties takes courage. When a rock lands on our head, when life brings us challenges, those challenges all serve the same core purpose, no matter what area of life they fall into. They all test our mental and emotional flexibility, and our willingness to learn and grow. It takes a much different level of awareness to carry us out of a difficult situation than it did to get us there.

Finding our way through a difficult situation is like walking between the walls of a maze. We may be moving forward, thinking that we're moving in the correct direction, but if we make a wrong turn we could find ourselves cornered. Fear keeps us in the corner and, through fear, we adapt our lives to stay in that corner. Courage keeps us moving forward, testing new channels and prodding new pathways. Every turn in life is a choice. Even the decision to do nothing is a choice. The maze is only a maze because we believe there are walls. Our choices and actions determine whether we stay in the maze or find our way out. Our choices and action determine whether we follow the walls or tear them down and use their stones to build bridges.

My self-rescue hike felt like a maze at first. My fears were its walls. To get on the trail I had to get out of my head and into my heart. I had to believe in possibilities. This was not easy. My emotional body was flooded with uncertainty. Yet I had to draw upon my deepest reservoir of inner strength to neutralize my fear with hope, love and courage. The emotional part of my rescue was the most difficult part of my day.

Whenever we are faced with difficulties, we instinctively respond with fear. After our initial response, we are given the choice to walk with courage or fear. When I became familiar with the seven laws, my understanding of fear and courage broadened tremendously. Through the law of polarity, I realized that fear and courage are different, yet very much the same. If we can feel fear, we can also feel courage. They are opposite emotions centered around the movement of going forward. The difference between the two is a matter of perspective. Courage is having positive expectations for an outcome, while fear is having negative expectations. Those expectations are based on our self-image, on past experiences of failure or success and on the way we use our imagination. If we are afraid of something, we use our imagination to create a negative image of the outcome. This creates the vibration of fear, amplifying all the destructive possibilities related to the object of our fear and drawing the related negative experience into our life. If we feel courageous about something, we use our imagination to create a positive image of the outcome. This creates the vibration of courage, which amplifies all the positive possibilities related to the object of our fear. We then draw the related positive results into our life.

One of the ways to increase our courage in any situation is to realize that we are projectors of thoughts and feelings. Our thoughts and feelings are energy that expands beyond our body and "arrives" in any given situation well before we arrive physically. Our beliefs about the outcome of a situation turn up before we do because we are energetically projecting the outcome in advance of our arrival. Our energy precedes us in the same way a cologne or perfume does. Often, a person's fragrance arrives in the room before he or she does, and it lingers after he or she leaves. The stronger and more concentrated the perfume or cologne, the stronger the fragrance before we arrive and after we leave. This is actually the reason we wear fragrances. We want to project an emotion or feeling about ourselves through the sense of smell before we arrive so that it has a positive effect on how others perceive us.

Our thoughts and feelings are made of the same energy as a fragrance, and they behave in a similar fashion. If we have positive expectations (courage) we will project a positive outcome. The forces of nature will align with the overall level of our courage, and our energy will arrive in the situation before we do. The stronger the "fragrance" of our courage, the more likely we are to attract a positive outcome. The strength of our emotional fragrance is based upon how fully we're able to use our feeling and imagination to empower our visualization. Most people are aware of the idea of projecting energy, but few understand how it works. People can sense our energy, our "fragrance" when they first see us. We say it all the time: "He has a good vibe," or "I don't like her vibe." We sense the energy because it is real.

When we are ready to follow the scent of our dreams, to make changes in our life, when we want to get out of a difficult situation, the scent of courage is the emotional antidote that takes us into new, unchartered territory. Courage is the vibration that helps us break out of our cocoon and spread our wings. It is by exercising courage that we take new risks and accumulate the new victories that ultimately build our self-confidence.

The amount of courage or fear we experience is a direct reflection of our emotional conditioning. The beautiful thing about courage is that sometimes we surprise ourselves and do things we didn't think we were capable of. This happens because what we are capable of is unlimited. And it usually takes a significant emotional event to push us past our fears and comfort zone and into a whole new level of inner strength. It also happens because our courage is based on our emotional references. It is our natural instinct to seek pleasure and avoid pain. The law of relativity allows us to look at two different choices and to choose the one that offers the least amount of pain. I was frightened by my injury and self-rescue. But the fear of loss from doing nothing gave me a boost of relative courage, which pushed me forward. This is the reason catastrophic events can be transformational: because we uncover and discover our hidden potential.

Courage is as much a choice as fear is because we always have a choice about which thoughts, emotions and beliefs to give our energy and attention to. We decide what things mean to us. The way things are is always related to our perception. Scary things do happen to us. But, ultimately, we always have the choice about what to focus on. The law of polarity gives us a lot of leverage when it comes to courage and fear. If something can be bad, it can also be good. This is not to deny painful experiences. It simply means that after the initial shock of an experience, the sooner we choose to look for the bright side, the sooner we can transmute the experience into something meaningful and beneficial.

In the moment I made the choice to stand up and begin hiking out, there is no doubt that I danced between fear and courage. However, I realized that if I followed my fears, I would give energy to them and they would be likely to come true. In that moment of decision, I realized that I could not afford a single negative thought. Courage was my only real choice.

Developing a high level of courage is one of the greatest gifts we can give to our self because it opens doors that can only be seen and experienced through a strong sense of self-worth. Life is a gift with a very short time span. Everything that happens between birth and death is a delicate dance of courage and fear. We all have ups and downs. Fear is our obstacle and courage is our walking stick. The magic and beauty in life comes when we realize how much influence we can have over our own fears if we understand the impact of our thoughts and beliefs. As we develop courage, self-confidence becomes our most familiar emotion, and fear becomes but a small hindrance to our positive expectations.

There's one small nuance that I learned from Anthony Robbins that is a shortcut to developing self-confidence and improving our lives: The questions we ask ourselves determine the thoughts we think and the answers we receive. We ask ourselves questions all day long. These questions can either build our self-esteem or perpetuate low self-image. If we ask a negative question ("Why can't I?"), we will get a disempowering answer. Likewise, if we ask a positive question (Why can I?"), we will get an empowering answer.

We are "meaning-makers." We can transmute any experience by changing the question we ask about it. The quality of the question determines the quality of the answer. Courage and self-confidence come from asking empowering questions: Why can I? What are my resources? Who can help me? How do I need to feel in order to make this happen?

It is important that we become consciously aware of the questions we are asking ourselves. It is equally importantly that we learn how to actively think. Thinking is the tool of the mind to create inner and outer experiences. It is the process of learning by asking questions and getting answers. Our mind always looks for answers to any question it is asked. If it doesn't have an answer, it will draw upon prior experiences or seek outside resources to come up with an answer. The answers are not always correct. The only way to measure them is by the results they create. If you are going to ask someone else for their opinion, make sure they have the results you want. If they don't, their opinion is of no value. The goal is to learn through thinking and asking proper questions. Courage and fear, ultimately, come from the quality of our thinking and the quality of our questions.

When a rock hits us on the head and life starts falling apart, it takes courage to ask positive, empowering questions and to see tragedy as a gift in disguise. It takes courage to tear down our walls and turn the stones into bridges. It takes courage to surrender blame and take total responsibility for our lives. It takes courage to look at our lives and realize how much of who we are has been influenced by our childhood. It takes courage to look life in the eye and reclaim our power over our conditioning and circumstances. It takes a tremendous amount of heart and courage to stand in the midst of our own battles, regardless of how things appear, and take total ownership of our thoughts, beliefs and emotions and begin to harvest goodness from tragedy.

All this courage and heart calls for the strength and a willingness to tap into our deepest, most hidden reservoir of personal power. If we truly want to chart a new course in life, it takes a firm decision, massive action, clarity of heart and mind and an untethered willingness to let go of old ideas. There are countless stories throughout the ages of people who have broken through the walls of tragedy, fear and adversity, who have overcome public resistance and scrutiny and launched a whole new life for themselves. Oprah Winfrey, Albert Einstein, Helen Keller, Michael Jordan, Walt Disney, Nelson Mandela, Mahatma Gandhi, are just a few of many familiar names.

Once we realize that we are all connected, once we realize that our thoughts and beliefs are the tools that sculpt our lives, once we grab onto the truth that we are not the victim of our story but, rather, the master of our destiny, then we can move forward with courage and determination toward our new horizons.

When I look back, my real fear was not of dying. My fear was that I hadn't lived enough, that I had not lived life to its fullest potential. My fear was that I had not loved enough and had not done enough to leave a positive legacy that would outlive me. I wasn't running from my injury or to the hospital. I was on a path of self-rescue because I wanted a second chance at life. My ticket back was courage.

What are you afraid of right now that is holding you back from fully living your potential? What is the rock in your life? What unrealized dreams are lingering in your heart and mind? What unwritten books are you holding onto? What greatness are you resisting? If you were to dig deep in your heart and mind, knowing that true faith (not blind faith) comes from understanding the laws of life, what would you be willing to let go of to return to the path of your heart, to the path of your dreams?

Within each of us is a champion, a man or woman with a dream. The ability to achieve that dream is there, inside every heart. Each of us has the ability to change our lives and have a deep and lasting impact on the world. Each of us has a unique talent and ability that, once we stop hiding behind our fears and excuses and tap into our reservoir of courage, can make the world a better place.

Remember the law of polarity. If you can be afraid, you can also be courageous. You have it in you. We all have it within us. We all have the courage to let go and move on. Don't wait for a rock — for an injury, for an illness or for someone you love to die. If you are not happy with the direction of your life today, then be proactive and take massive action today. Only you can make the changes in your life that you want. There is no lifeguard on the journey of life, except your own choices and actions.

Change takes courage. You have it in you! We all do! We all have the laws of life on our side. We all have the full power of the universe waiting in the wings to help us move forward. All we need to do is let go of the fear-vibes that hold us back and tap into the wave of energy that gives us strength and courage.

Do it now! Tomorrow is never promised.

FOURTEEN

Awareness

He who learns but does not think, is lost!
He who thinks but does not learn is in great danger.
~ Confucius

THROUGH MY RETURN TO CHACO CANYON, I realized that even though we are here to have our own unique journey, an untethered approach to life does not negate the consequences of our actions. The law of cause and effect is always operating. Everything we do has an overall effect on life. We are a part of life, not apart from it. In each moment we have an opportunity to make choices that are either empowering or destructive, choices that affect our life and the overall wellbeing of humanity.

The human journey is largely a mystery. With all life's possibilities for beauty, love, romance, happiness, creativity and wonderful experiences, there is still the other extreme of war, political and religious battles and the destruction of our planet and many of its indigenous tribes and cultural beliefs — all in the name of progress or God.

The law of gender is very clear that all thoughts have a natural incubation period before they can manifest. If you look at the overall condition of humanity, it's easy to see what we have been thinking about and focusing on. We have made a lot of destructive choices that are now becoming so obvious that most of the world is trying to figure out what happened and how we got here. The effect of these choices is the equivalent of a rock having landed on the head of humanity. The wound has been slowly hemorrhaging and festering for some time. Now we are looking at our world with shock and disgust.

As much as I enjoyed the beauty of Chaco Canyon, one of the many thoughts circulating in my mind before the rock clipped me was my concern over the "virus" plaguing humanity, the virus of ignorance, laziness and arrogance.

❖ Our ignorance of who we truly are and what we are capable of, as individuals and collectively as humanity.

❖ Our lazy attitude toward our personal power and genetic potential.

❖ Our arrogance that we believe we can bomb one part of the planet and not have it affect the entire planet.

❖ Our arrogance that we believe there is no relationship between what we think and eat, and the overall quality of our physical, mental and emotional health.

❖ Our arrogance that we believe it's okay, as individuals or collectively as humanity, to treat people, ourselves and the earth the way we do.

Standing amidst the remnants of a lost and missing culture can be a painful reminder that what we are doing to ourselves and our planet through ignorance, arrogance and laziness could easily create the same outcome for us that it did for the Anasazi. As much as I see the beauty in life, I also realize the growing concerns of humanity. Of course, it's important that we learn to look for the opportunity in difficulties, that we give energy and attention to solutions rather than problems. But not everyone has the physical, mental and emotional strength, courage and awareness to look past appearances. When people are starving to death, when people are in the midst of painful injuries or disease or in a war's crossfire, when people experience any other rock-on-the head, it can hard to be hopeful for change.

For those of us more fortunate when it comes to the quality of our lives, as we embrace the laws of energy and the truth that we are one people sharing one planet, it becomes our duty to share our awareness and help those less fortunate by reaching out with compassion and discernment. The compassion comes from understanding that we are all seeking to love and be loved. The discernment comes from recognizing that we cannot help people who do not want to be helped. Some people have to hit bottom before they are willing to open up to new thoughts and ideas. It is not our responsibility to rescue people who are not asking to be rescued. Our duty is to spread awareness through the example of our life so that all humanity can grow into being self-sustaining and self-reliant.

It is difficult to watch people suffer. Yet we can't know what is best for others. Only they can know, through their own experiences and their own suffering. We each have our own path. We can only work on our own awareness. Through our own expansion, those who are ready for help will recognize the light that is shining from within us, and the laws of vibration and attraction will bring us together. Our responsibility is to garden our heart and our mind, to cultivate a more peaceful world through our actions and choices, and to contribute love and goodness in the moment. Our responsibility is to be a living demonstration of the power of consistent thought, to help people who want to be helped, and to create and give energy to situations that will bring about change in a powerful, meaningful and lasting way.

As much as I talk about love and gratitude, I do so because my intention is to inspire people to let go of their fears and doubts and explore the far-reaching possibilities that come from courage and global awareness. It's time to start paying attention to the bigger picture. It's time to be honest with ourselves about the way things are, and what we are truly capable of. It's time to tear down the walls, pick up the torch and start restoring our planet and reclaiming the heart and soul of humanity. This is not about handouts. This is about waking up from our self-induced hypnosis and taking responsibility for ourselves and the direction of humanity

When you remove the filter of the media and peel away the distractions of day-to-day-life, the overall condition of humanity is shamefully degraded. There is a mental and emotional dis-ease of pandemic proportions that is causing us to destroy ourselves and is destroying the hearts and lives of millions of people across the globe. The reality is that most people on the planet are severely deprived of love, self-worth and the basic necessities of life. This deprivation is a symptom of a misunderstanding of who and what we are, individually and collectively, and what we are capable of. This symptom causes us to surrender our authority over our own lives to a false belief about ourselves. Because of this false belief, we have chosen to give away our personal power, our ability to live, love and create, to the handful of people who lead the world through destructive and degrading social and political paradigms. The world we live in now is a shadow of who we are and what we are capable of.

The self-worth of humanity is so degraded that most people look for love and significance in all the wrong places. People fill the emotional gap with food, toys, drugs, alcohol, shopping, serial dating or false starts at love and relationship. Most of humanity has become completely wrapped up in the external feedback of how other people perceive them, rather than how they see themselves. Even though we crave a life abundant with love, joy and prosperity, many people falsely believe that we can achieve these by following social and cultural norms that define us externally, rather than by knowing who we are from the inside out.

There is no reason for anyone to live in deprivation of love, self-worth, friendship or the basic necessities of life. There is no reason for anyone to trade their uniqueness and individuality for conformity and control. There is no reason to raise children in fear and to perpetuate the lie of learned helplessness and victim-consciousness. With all our resources, there is no reason for people to live in filth and disease. There is no reason other that we have forgotten who we are. We have forgotten that we are a part of nature, not apart from it. We have forgotten because we were never taught the truth.

The truth is, the world is not out of balance. Everything is happening according to law. The real issue is not distribution of wealth, but a lack of awareness of who and what we truly are. We were never taught the laws of energy or the faculties of our mind. We were never taught the truth that even though we are different, we are the same at our core. This lack of awareness reflects outwardly as poverty, lack, limitation and disease. Humanity is not living in emotional or financial poverty because of a lack of resources, but because humanity has kept itself ignorant of the most fundamental laws of life. Humanity lives this way because the collective story of everyone on this planet, the collective consciousness of all of humanity, has become one of poverty, lack and limitation.

- ❖ Lack of health.
- ❖ Lack of love.
- ❖ Lack of romance.
- ❖ Lack of friends.
- ❖ Lack of confidence.
- ❖ Lack of time.
- ❖ Lack of opportunity.
- ❖ Lack of happiness.
- ❖ Lack of money.
- ❖ Lack of awareness.

All this lack, all this poverty consciousness, comes from the simple truth that we are conditioned from childhood to think and live from the outside in, rather than the inside out. Our ignorance of the laws of energy and the faculties of our mind lead us to believe that life is something that happens to us rather than something we co-create with our natural-born abilities. Wealth is a state of mind. Wealth is not about having. It is about thinking and feeling in a certain way. It is about focusing on what we want and giving it an emotional charge, as if it already exists, rather than focusing on the way things appear outwardly at the moment. If we focus on and give our energy and attention to what we don't want, we create more of what we don't want. The law of cause and effect makes it very clear. We cannot create something by focusing on its opposite. We cannot live a wealthy life by focusing on poverty, lack and limitation. Nature is abundant. There is no poverty or lack according to universal laws, except that which we create through what we give our attention to — through our own thoughts, beliefs, emotions and actions, through social conditioning and through our choice to empower a socio-economic system that breeds poverty, mediocrity and humanitarian injustice.

Wealth is all-encompassing. Financial riches are only a small part of the tree of wealth. We all seek a wealth of love, happiness, friends, opportunity, time, romance, adventure, health and money, along with countless expressions of abundance. Ultimately, the wealth that we experience in every area of life is a reflection of our awareness of what we believe is possible to have and experience in our own life. If a person is financially broke, or living in financial poverty, the problem is not a lack of money. That is the symptom. The problem is poverty consciousness. To increase wealth, we have to alter our awareness and our beliefs. We have to elevate our consciousness to abundance.

The challenges of the world are self-evident, but the laws of energy are not. It doesn't take much to become aware of the social and humanitarian injustices that plague humanity. They're right here in our face. Likewise, it doesn't take much to learn and understand the laws of energy or the faculties of the mind. What it does take is a willingness to expand our awareness and open our hearts and minds to new thoughts and ideas about who we are and what we are capable of. When we learn, embrace and apply the seven natural laws, when we understand and correctly utilize the faculties of our mind, when we take total responsibility for the conditions of the world, including the conditions of our own life, then we will be ready to raise our standards about what is and isn't acceptable as a global community. From there, it will take sincere heart and courage to let go of ideas and beliefs that no longer serve us and to replace them with new, empowering choices.

We always have a choice. We can use our thoughts, feelings and actions to perpetuate the lie of poverty, lack and limitation. Or we can use the same energy and laws to explore the outer limits of our mind and imagination to create a truly abundant life.

We deserve to live a happy, prosperous, abundant life. We deserve to eat quality foods, to enjoy beautiful art, to travel to distant lands and learn about different cultures. We deserve to live in the home of our dreams and to live our dream lifestyle. We deserve this, because we are creative beings who are immersed in an infinite supply of energy and are naturally connected to the laws of energy. It is our responsibility to become aware of the laws and to utilize them in our day-to-day life.

None of us is alone on this planet. At this writing, there are nearly seven billion people who make up the global community. Even though only a few thousand run the governments of the world, this is not a game of "us versus them." Those few thousand people are also a part of our global community. They have harnessed the paradigm of fear and are perpetuating the dis-ease of poverty, lack and limitation because we as a global community have made the choice to live this way, either by ignorance or laziness. Through this choice, we have drawn into our global experience leaders with intentions that appear to be less than benevolent. They have done nothing wrong. We are not the victims of government or unfair laws. We are not the victims of war or political unrest. We are not the victims of poverty, plague, famine or disease. We are totally responsible for what is going on throughout our entire planet. We are responsible by choice and neglect. We are responsible because the laws of energy that work on the individual level also work on the global level.

The tables will turn in our favor only when humanity awakens to the truth that we have given our power away through our collective consciousness of fear, lack and limitation...when we reawaken our hearts and our imagination...when we start thinking for ourselves rather than allowing the media to think for us...when we stop believing that we need to be rescued by the government...when we stop thinking in terms of separation and realize we are all connected...when we stop sucking on the breast of social welfare and government entitlements...when we see that we are giving our power away...when we understand that the laws of energy are here to serve us, not enslave us. All of this can be done peacefully, by being aware of the problems and focusing on solutions.

Our solutions start in our own heart and mind, then expand outwardly into our family, community, nation and global community. They start when we realize that we live in an abundant universe with an infinite supply of energy and resources to create anything that wants to be created. They start with simple coffee-talk. They start when we meet our neighbors and create a sense of community by doing things together to improve our neighborhood. They start when we start being friendly with the people with whom we interact on a daily basis. They start when we look at what we have in common rather than at what separates us. They start when we make better choices about the food we eat and the products we consume and discard. They start when we pay attention to our thoughts and beliefs, pulling the weeds and sowing new, positive and empowering ideas. They start when we discard our self-limiting, self-defeating story and create a new, empowering one. They start when we realize that behind every set of eyes is the same power and force that created each of us. Behind every set of eyes is an individualized expression of the entire fabric of energy and life.

Our solutions start with gratitude, courage, forgiveness and total responsibility. They start right here, right now.

This entire planet is in pain, living with the residual effects of a belief system based on controlling hearts and minds through fear. Everyone wants freedom. But true freedom does not come from our ability to say yes to what we want. It comes from the courage, strength and ability to say no to that which we know will destroy us.

Humanity is like a caterpillar. We have the potential to fly like a butterfly. But first we must be willing to let go of our current thoughts and limiting beliefs, enter the cocoon of change and emerge with our newfound freedom. What is it going to take for us to wake up, break out of our cocoon, spread our wings and reclaim our personal power? How much longer are we going to sit around hoping, praying, begging and pretending? How much longer are we going to stay drunk with fear? How much longer are we going to hide behind the veil of learned helplessness and victim consciousness? How much longer are we going to listen to the media and believe that war is peace and debt is abundance? How much longer are we going to believe that we can love someone else without loving ourselves?

What is going to be your turning point? When are you going to take massive action to clean up your life? When are you going to let go of your unhealthy emotional entanglements and take responsibility for your body, your health, your thoughts, your actions and your beliefs? When are you going to stop feeding your mind and body with garbage and start listening to the voice of your heart? When are you going to wake up from the illusion that there is a whopping gap between you, your thoughts and your experiences in life? There is no gap. Everything is connected. Every thought is a cause. Every thought is a seed. The life we see outside of us first started inside us.

A falling rock landed on my head and opened my heart. A rock has also fallen on the heart of humanity. I pray that you see and feel the depth of the wound. The people of this earth are ready for a massive self-rescue mission.

The hearts of the world are begging for fresh answers to problems that have been getting the same bandage for thousands of years. The answers are here. Do you have the courage to step out as a leader, to open your heart, to change your story, to take total responsibility for your life, to turn your walls into bridges and to restore the bridge between your heart and mind? You do! We all do!

The problems of our world offer us our greatest opportunities. Now more than ever, we have the technology and resources to make a difference in a peaceful, positive and meaningful way. We have reached a point in time where the crack in the dam that holds back our creative potential and all of our personal power can no longer be plugged and painted over. Fear may have brought us to this moment. But courage, creativity and imagination is what will give birth to the renewed heart and spirit of humanity.

I pray that my rock opens your heart and mind as it did mine and that it gives you the courage and strength to chart a new course for your life. I pray that you take that courage, study and learn the laws, and reconnect with the truth that we are all connected. Whatever we do to one, we do to all. Together as one people, we can restore health and freedom to the hearts and lives of humanity.

The possibility for this freedom is real. I saw it on that desert plateau. I saw it in the sand, pebbles, stones and rocks of Chaco Canyon. The sand comes from pebbles. The pebbles come from stones. The stones come from rocks. And the rocks come from larger fallen chunks of the big rock walls. Even though things are always falling apart, there is no such thing as destruction. There is only change. The experience of life will always change. Whether in my lifetime or not, humanity will eventually wake up to the truth that we are all one, that there is no separation, and all the walls of fear and limitation will crumble to the ground.

One by one, we are waking up.

FIFTEEN

A Moment In Time

As a single footstep will not make a path on the earth, so a single thought will not make a pathway in the mind. To make a deep physical path, we walk again and again. To make a deep mental path, we must think over and over the kind of thoughts we wish to dominate our lives.
   ~ *Henry David Thoreau*

THE CANVAS OF LIFE is as broad and wide as can be imagined. With all the possibilities of life, it is amazing how much can be seen within the confines of the desert. Through my eyes I was seeing the big picture. I was seeing the faces of nature, the rocks, the sage, the sky, the sunshine and all the ancient ruins. I was seeing how everything was separate yet connected.

I stopped, closed my eyes and reflected upon all my thoughts of the day. I thought about how all of life is organized by law, how we are all made of energy and how we are all energetically connected. I thought about the power of our mind, of the dream-weavers and dream-stealers, and of the importance of responsibility, forgiveness and gratitude. I thought about the collage of life and the vibrations of fear, struggle and courage. I thought about awareness and about the tremendous opportunity we have to change the impressions of the world. As I reflected upon all these thoughts, I thought about the power of a minute.

Every minute of life has unlimited value. In one minute a poem can be written that will touch people's hearts and lives forever. In one minute we can smile, sing and dance. In one minute we can encourage someone, forgive someone or comfort someone. In one minute we can inspire someone with creative ideas and celebrate life with an abundance of joy. In one minute we can make someone laugh. In one minute we can change the world. Because in one minute we can change thoughts and change our beliefs.

The beauty of life is found in every increment of time because it is here, in the moment, that all decisions are made. It is in the moment that we decide what energy to tap into, which thoughts to focus on and which feelings to give energy to. It is right here in this moment that we shape our lives. All life experiences begin with thought. And it is right here, right now, that we choose our thoughts.

Each moment is delicate. So much can be gained and lost simply by our moment-to-moment choices. There is unlimited power and potential in the moment. The smallest amount of water can make the biggest difference in the beauty and strength of a flower. One smile can send ripples of love and happiness across the world. A simple hug can completely change the direction of a person's day. The food we eat can nourish or poison us. The air we breathe can kill us or make us strong. The words we speak can be used to encourage and inspire or belittle and destroy. We can tell people we love them or we can show them. All of this is done in the moment. Every choice we make occurs right here, right now.

When we look at the conditions of the moment, when we look at "what is," we are looking at the residual effects of past choices and actions. Everything we do and say in this moment creates its own set of circumstances, actions and reactions. Every thought we have is a seed of a whole new potential reality. When the seed is planted, nourished and cultivated, it creates a new world of possibilities. Everything affects everything. There is a web of energy that connects all things. Whatever we do to the web in this moment in time, we do to ourselves. Every action creates a reaction. This is the beauty of the moment. We never have to wait for it to arrive. It is in this very moment that we choose our destiny, by way of the choices we make, the thoughts we sow and the actions we take. All this occurs and begins, right here, right now. There is nothing to wait for. There is nothing to hold onto. Do not wait to let go. Do not wait to forgive. Do not wait to love. Do not wait to laugh. Do not wait to live. Everything starts right here. Everything starts right now. We aren't on the road to nowhere. We are on the road to now-here.

The power of the moment is the power to create. We are simple creatures with simple needs to love, laugh, contribute and evolve. Our ability to fulfill our dreams comes from our power to choose our thoughts, beliefs and actions. No matter what our story is, no matter what happened in the past, each moment is a chance to start a new life by letting go of our past and choosing a new set of thoughts, beliefs and actions. The only things we ever have to hold onto are the things we are afraid to let go of. It is our responsibility to choose what we hold onto and let go of and to decide what to do with each moment. Everything we have done up until now — good, bad or ugly — has been nothing more than training and preparation for the next moment in time.

Life is a treasure hunt. Time is our game board and our opportunity. Everything we seek exists. There are hidden treasures to be found, but they will not be found in the past or the future. They will only be found here and now. Humanity is looking for the treasure. We are looking for the one person, place, thing or idea that will fill our treasure chest and set us free. There is no freedom outside our own thoughts and beliefs. We can never be free as long as we are slaves and hostages to our thoughts and fears about the past or the future, slaves to the illusion that we are powerless and helpless. As long as we live in fear, we can never discover our treasure, we can never discover the transformational power of a moment in time.

All the treasures of life can be uncovered through the power of courage, through the power of a decision, through the power of being completely present and aware of who and what we are, right here and right now. Our ability to make decisions is what allows these treasures to be discovered. The universe will always reflect into our lives what we love and fear, and the experiences we need in order to learn and grow. The treasures are hidden in the moment, often disguised behind difficulties and challenges. But they are all here, now, waiting to be discovered.

There is no treasure chest outside our own hearts and minds.

- ❖ We are the ones who decide whether we will have a positive or negative attitude toward life.
- ❖ We are the ones who decide what to think about and focus on.
- ❖ We are the ones who decide whether we experience wealth and abundance or poverty, lack and limitation.
- ❖ We are the ones who decide whether we experience health, energy, fitness and vitality or weakness, illness and disease.
- ❖ We are the ones who decide whether we will lead or follow.
- ❖ We are the ones who decide whether we will have high standards or low standards.
- ❖ We are the ones who decide whether we will learn and grow or remain stagnant and complacent.
- ❖ We are the ones who decide whether we will have faith and courage, or live in fear.
- ❖ We are the ones who decide whether we will forgive others or hold onto anger and resentment.
- ❖ We are the ones who decide whether we will live joyfully or fearfully.
- ❖ We are the ones who decide whether we will make changes in our life or continue with old patterns.
- ❖ We are the ones who decide whether we will live in love or in anger and self-pity.

- ❖ We are the ones who decide whether our experiences are good or bad, meaningful or superficial.
- ❖ We are the ones who give power to our story and who have the power to change our story.
- ❖ We are the ones who choose the nature of our friendships and relationships.
- ❖ We are the ones who choose whether or not our dreams will come true.
- ❖ We are the ones who choose what will stop us and what will keep us moving forward.
- ❖ We are the ones who create walls or bridges.
- ❖ We are the ones who decide if there is peace on earth.

There is no one stopping us but ourselves. There is nothing stopping us but our own thoughts and limiting beliefs. There is no one to blame for anything. There is no one who can love us more than we love ourselves. When we open to learning the laws of life and the nature of our mind, we open the door to infinite possibilities.

We are the ones. There is no other.

I am the one. You are the one. We are the ones.

There is only one field of energy, and we are it!

Tatvamasi (Thou Art That)

SIXTEEN

Gratitude Is Everything

Show me the path of gratitude. Show me the gratitude in all of my adversity. Show me the gratitude in all of my misery. Show me the gratitude in all of my pain. Show me the gratitude in all of my curiosity. Show me the gratitude in all of my pleasure. Show me the gratitude in all of my happiness. Show me the gratitude in every thought, word, deed, experience and journey.

Open my heart, mind and soul, and show me the gratitude that will restore balance to my life. Restore the fire of passion within my heart and soul, fueled by my feelings to do, be and achieve my very best. Show me the gratitude in a smile, in a flower, in a drop of water, in the chirp of a bird. Show me the way of gratitude in everything I do, see, hear, touch, smell and feel. Show me how to say, thank you to all of life, to everything.

~ David Lloyd Strauss

I FINALLY MADE IT BACK to the Pueblo Bonito overlook, a part of the trail that will always hold a deep and meaningful place in my heart. I took a moment to breathe in the air and absorb the view. My flood of emotions returned. I sat down, crossed my legs, buried my face in my hands and started crying.

Two years earlier, my tears had been tears of despair. I had arrived here, my head, face and body encrusted with blood, in hopeful anticipation of being found and rescued. Yet no one had been around. I thought my time had expired. I never imagined that I would return. Yet here I was, again in tears. This time, though, my tears were tears of gratitude.

As I sat there, I fell into a complete state of gratitude and began reviewing everything that I was grateful for. They are the same things I'm still grateful for today.

I am grateful for my physical, mental and emotional healing.

I am grateful for all the lessons I have learned and for the gift of being able to share them with the world.

I am grateful to be freed from the shackles of my past and for the gift of a whole new life.

I am grateful for all the pain I have been through because it has taught me the power of courage, forgiveness and responsibility.

I am grateful for the mountains, rivers, streams and valleys...for all the critters and creatures of life...for the sunrises and sunsets...for the full moon and the new moon.

I am grateful for the courage to love and be loved...for all my friends and family, for all the happy memories and for all the times of loving and sharing.

I am grateful for the incredible life with which I have been blessed, for all the light and love that flows through my days, and for all the wonderful people who have touched my heart.

I am grateful for the awareness that we are all one and that we are all energetically connected through the power and vibration of love.

I am truly grateful for the gift of a healthy body: for eyes that see, ears that hear, a nose that smells, skin that allows me to experience texture and temperature, and a mouth through which I can speak and taste.

I am grateful for all the organs and systems of my body: a heart that pumps my blood, a brain that processes the experience of life, lungs that allow me to breathe, a circulatory system that delivers oxygen and nutrition to my cells, and a nervous system that connects my inner and outer worlds.

I am grateful for the gift of time.

Above all, I am grateful for the gift of life, and for the greatest gift that can be imagined: a second chance at life.

I am grateful for everyone and everything.

Gratitude offers all a person could ask for. Gratitude offers peace, happiness, a quiet mind, certainty of purpose and a sense of self-worth that transcends all perceived limitations.

Gratitude is the sparkle in our eyes, the joy in our hearts and the happiness and peace that illuminate the path of life.

Gratitude is the single most powerful resource available to humanity. Gratitude is like sunshine to a flower. It brings out its color, luster and beauty. When our life is filled with gratitude, we experience all the color and magnitude of the power of love. All the riches in the universe are quickly uncovered in a continuous state of gratitude.

The vibration of gratitude is the valve that opens the floodgates to all the abundance found through the law of cause and effect. Gratitude is mental and emotional alchemy. It is the law of transmutation in action. Through the power of love, gratitude can transmute any thought and experience into something beautiful, meaningful and abundant.

Gratitude is an expression of love, and love is a gift that can only be received when given. Gratitude is being thankful for what we have, regardless of how much or how little we have. Gratitude will carry us further along our journey than any other wind that blows in our sails. When we live in a place of gratitude, we open to the possibility of increase in every area of life. A grateful heart and mind is a magnet to goodness. By living in a place of gratitude, we align our thoughts and emotions with the energetic forces of the universe, which then draw the parallel of our desires into our life.

Gratitude goes beyond simple thanks. It is more than a simple word. It extends into the depths of our heart and the power of our mind. To live in sincere gratitude is to understand, live and dance with the laws of energy.

When we understand the laws of cause and effect, gender, transmutation, polarity, relativity, vibration and rhythm, we understand that gratitude is the magnet that brings all the laws into harmonic cooperation.

When we understand the law of vibration, we see that by consistently holding onto a thought filled with positive emotions, we increase the amplitude of the vibration related to that thought, which increases its magnetic power and speeds up the rate at which we draw the experience into our life.

When we understand the law of polarity, we see that we do not need to make decisions based on the way things appear at the moment, because the moment is simply a residue of the past. The law of polarity allows us to look at the way things are, the conditions that we want to move away from. It then allows us to visualize their opposite and create a new image and feeling focused on our desired direction and outcome. Gratitude is the vacuum that pulls us out of that residue and draws all new possibilities into our life. It is the gateway that opens the flow of miracles.

When we lack gratitude, we lack everything. If we experience poverty or lack in any area of our life, it is because we lack gratitude in that area. The law of cause and effect makes it very clear. In order for any result (effect) to take form, it must first have a cause. It must be initiated with a clear image in our mind and consistent thoughts and feelings, believing it to be real before it has actually become real. Just as gratitude draws all possibilities into our life, a lack of gratitude creates the resistance that prevents the flow of abundance. By living in gratitude, we choose the meaning we give to this moment in time. We see this moment, regardless of what has happened or appears to be happening, as fertile soil to plant new seeds of thought.

Gratitude is the eternal elixir. It is the potion for all problems and the serum for success. It is the antidote to poverty and the highway to healing. When we feel grateful for what we desire with the same intensity as if we already had it, we unleash powerful energetic forces that will flood our life with miracles.

To be grateful is to be truly obedient to the law of gender. We cannot have faith and doubt at the same time. Gratitude loves consistency. Everything takes time. To allow gratitude to fully bless our life, we have to allow our dreams and desires to align in their own time.

To live in a place of gratitude takes courage. All our personal power is found in this moment in time, not in the past or future. How we think and feel during this moment in time is what creates the energy that defines the next moment in time and activates what will manifest in our life down the road. Thoughts of gratitude should be our first thoughts in the morning and the lullaby that we sing to ourselves at night.

When I was hiking myself out, my dance with different emotions was the law of rhythm in action. Yet, it was my words and feelings of gratitude that ultimately became the wind in my sails of survival. When I reached that moment of despair on the Pueblo Bonito overlook I was emotionally broken, yet I could no longer afford any negative thoughts. It was do or die. Ultimately, it was my prayer of surrender and gratitude that restored my strength and reinvigorated my soul.

Bob Proctor shares a simple and powerful phrase that is the potion to living in a place of gratitude. No matter what we want in life, we begin the process of creation by using these eight words in relation to our thoughts and feelings: "I am so happy and grateful now that..." This simple phrase activates the laws by empowering the moment as a point of transition and creation, rather than as an anchor to our past.

I am so happy and grateful now that I am healed. I am so happy and grateful now that I am sharing the beauty of the power of gratitude.

After everything I've been through, I finally discovered the single key that opens the door to the hidden treasures of life. Of all the emotions we experience, gratitude is the one that is the foundation for activating the truth of abundance. Gratitude is everything!

SEVENTEEN

Seeing The Unseen

Love is the gift of happiness and caring.
Let us give of our hearts to those who need sharing.
Our love has no end as it has no beginning.
It has always been part of us and joys in being given.
With our love comes the desire to give and receive,
For love flows freely and is a gift indeed.
~ David Lloyd Strauss

MY TEARS OF GRATITUDE at the Pueblo Bonito overlook were like a day at the spa for my thoughts and emotions. They cleansed my heart and soul and refreshed my mind. When I was done, I picked myself up and continued on.

This time, I saw the unseen.

The most powerful forces in the world are invisible to the human eye: light, wind, air, temperature, electricity and time.

We see the effects of their power, demonstrated as the beauty of nature and the experiences in our life. Yet their power is unseen.

We see the effects of light, as flowers reach for the heavens and rainbows dance across a rain-filled sky. Yet light is unseen.

We see the effects of wind, as trees bend to their movement and canyons form from their powerful forces. Yet wind is unseen.

We see the effects of air, as we inhale each breath and witness the life-giving power of this magical force. Yet air is unseen.

We see the effects of heat, as we enjoy a sunny afternoon, feeling the warmth on our skin. Yet heat is unseen.

We see the effects of cold, as moisture crystallizes on our nose during a crisp winter afternoon. Yet cold is unseen.

We see the effects of electricity, as we light our homes or smell the scent of cooking food. Yet electricity is unseen.

The laws of life are also unseen, yet the results of how we use these laws also show up in our lives: as our experiences.

We do not see with our naked eyes that everything is made of energy. Yet when we look closely at the collage of life, it is energy that makes up everything.

Love, too, is unseen. It does not have a face, yet we see its effects in our experiences of our life.

Love is who we are. Love is everywhere. It is in our hearts, in the sun, in the rain and in the oceans, beaches, mountains, rivers and sky. It is in the child on the swing, the smile of a puppy and the song of a lovebird.

Love is the very essence that defines all of existence. It is the one ingredient that unites all things.

We see the gifts, the smiles, the laughter, the intimacy and the gentle touch of someone we love. Yet love is unseen.

We feel the warmth of an embrace during difficult times and experience leaps of joy during the best of times.

There are endless signs that love is in our life. Yet love is unseen.

Love is our true nature. It is not something we will find through another person or experience. It cannot be found in a book, atop a mountain or in the sea. It cannot be found through a drug, food or substance, through religion, sex or music. These may be paths on the quest for love but, in the end, all the love we seek can only be found within. Love is not something that we fall into or out of. It is what we are.

Love is the most powerful and inspiring energy in the world because love is the vibration of life. In the words of Mother Theresa, "The greatest poverty in the world is to die feeling unloved." To die feeling unloved would be to die with no idea or feeling of who and what we truly are.

We are all teachers and students of the study of love. What we seek is the simplicity of knowing who we are, of loving and accepting ourselves and of pursuing our own creativity. Through reaching out into other people's lives, we learn to reach within and discover our own greatness. Using the sword of courage, we cut through our fog of fear and uncertainty so that our quest can come full circle, so that we can return to an understanding that, whatever our outward adventures, the love that we seek can only be found within.

We are one people. One ocean. One earth. One sky. One body of energy. Though the thread that unites us is unseen, we are all connected. We are not here only for ourselves. We are also here for each other. It is time to remember the simplicity of life: that the greatest gift we can give to the world is to be ourselves! A flower gives to the beauty of an open field simply by being. We, too, need not try to give. All we need to do is be who and what we are, our authentic self. When we do that, our unseen greatness comes to life, and we brighten the world for all of life's creation.

We are living the gift of time. Time is infinite beauty. It is a never ending cycle of beginnings and endings. Time is that space that is both measurable and immeasurable. We don't know when it begins and we don't know when it ends. We just know that we are...you are...I am.

With time, we are given choices about how to live our lives — what to do, what to think, where to go, how to respond, whom to love, how to love. Time is the most valuable gift we can receive. With it we have the choice of how to define our life.

Love is the pure energy of life. Love is eternal. The impressions of love that we leave after we die will impact all of eternity. We can never run out of love. But we will run out of time. A lifetime is a limited canvas upon which to paint the thoughts and dreams of our heart and mind. Time passes quickly...too quickly. We never know when a life will end. Do not take time for granted. Learn to embrace the moment. Learn to live with love — right here, right now.

Time is our greatest and most valuable resource. It is the one gift we can give that can never be replaced or returned. We can replace money. We can replace clothing. But we can never regain time. I was given a second serving of time. I don't know how long it will last. What I do know now is the value and importance of grasping the full power and potential of each moment in time.

There are many journeys we will take in life, but none is longer than the journey from head to heart. We can spend all the time of our life looking for answers outside of ourselves. But everything we desire is found only within the chambers of our own heart and mind.

Whatever your strengths and weaknesses, do not hesitate to embrace all that life has to offer. Look within. Love your life just as you are! Embrace life. Embrace opportunities to learn and grow. Let the light within you shine outwardly — live it and love it!

Live and love with passion and affection. Put your heart into everything you do, even brushing your teeth. Whether you are petting your dog or cat or expressing love to your partner, friends or family, do it with boundless affection. You never know when a life or situation will end. So give to each moment your all, and leave a powerful legacy of love and affection.

Love people by bringing out the best in them. Be creative and thoughtful toward others. It's not enough to speak love. Show it in everything you do. Show it in small ways and big ways. Show it with passion, with surprise and with affection. Show it with gifts, with hugs, with kisses, with smiles, with laughter, with chocolate, with imagination.

Be authentic and creative. Share your love for life, people and the world in your own unique way, even if it comes across as being crazy and outrageous. It's worth it!

It doesn't take much to spread goodness around the world. Life is pregnant with endless possibilities. We are surrounded by pure potential. It is found in the trees, the birds, the monkeys, the moon, the sun, the rivers, the fish and the sea. It is within us and amongst us. It is everywhere, and we are it!

Be an expression of the unseen power of love!

Live and love with passion!

EIGHTEEN

Let It Be

When one door closes another door opens; but we often look so long and so regretfully upon the closed door that we do not see the ones which open for us.
~ *Alexander Graham Bell*

WITH EAGER ANTICIPATION, I finally arrived within a few hundred yards of the place of the rock fall. Just as I was stepping onto the trail, I looked down and saw footprints in the sand. They were not mine this time. But when I saw them, my energy shifted. My entire body tingled and a knot grew in my belly. I was on the same trail where I had found my footsteps after the fall. Ever since that day, footprints on a dirt or sand trail remind me how a simple impression saved my life.

When I began my return hike earlier in the day, I was set on returning to the exact place of my injury. Now that I was close, my feelings changed. Somehow, it felt as though returning to that spot would be like entering into an open tomb and violating a sacred space. A part of me died that day, and I wanted to let it rest in peace. Some things are best left alone. I sat down on the dirt trail, surrounded by sage, juniper and desert flowers, closed my eyes, took a deep breath, found a quiet place in my heart and mind, and reflected upon what all this really meant to me.

I thought about three lines in a poem I once wrote.

Touch A Rock, Touch The Past.
Touch A Flower, Touch The Present.
Touch A Heart, Touch Eternity.

I had touched a rock, and it touched me. The flowers that now surrounded me were beautiful desert flowers, but they could not last. They would eventually return to the soil to become nourishment for future generations.

A rock had fallen on my head and opened my heart. Since that day, my heart has been touched in meaningful and profound ways, and my story of that experience will touch eternity.

My journey on the upper plateau had transformed my life. I used to think something was missing from my life. It was me that was missing. I got lost in my own thoughts and fears and went wandering through the walled maze of my own story. The reality is that life has always been here for me. All I ever had to do was let go of my fears, build a bridge between my heart and mind, and extend that bridge across to the heart and mind of all of life. The journey between my heart and mind was the longest journey I have ever taken.

Before the rock fall, I did not know or understand the seven laws. I certainly did not understand the depth to which our thoughts impact our lives. As a result, I had a lot of anger, resentment and blame. It is so easy to blame others for our problems and challenges. It is so easy to look outwardly for something or someone to blame. Yet the laws of life teach us to look within, to seek inwardly the flaws in our own character. They teach us to look within because there is no truth outside our own heart, mind and soul. Life is an inner journey that expresses outwardly as the experiences of our life. Our life is always a reflection of our thoughts, beliefs and actions.

Sometimes, as Hawkwind once taught me, we cannot find out who we are until we realize who we are not. Now, finally, I can embrace that teaching. It is by wandering in the darkness that we discover the light. The farther we move away from truth, the closer we come to understanding it. It is by expanding our relationship to the outer world and by journeying amidst and beyond our fears that we come to know and understand the laws of life. As we reach out into the relationships of the physical world and as we test the laws of life, we are actually reaching within. Because who we are, the reflections of energy and love that we are, is mirrored in the form of physical experience. The more we listen to and learn from experience, the more we learn about ourselves. It is as if life were a game of hide-and-go-seek, and we return home through the journey of discovering the hidden laws of life, the laws hidden in our very own hearts and minds.

I looked again at the footprints on the trail and realized that we are all exactly where we need to be in life, exactly where the choices we have made and our understanding of life have carried us. Good choices or bad, we each act out the beliefs we hold to be true. Every step in the sand is a movement in the direction of our beliefs. Every adversity and blessing is of our own making because we are co-creators in life's web of experience. The only thing we can control is our thoughts and actions in the moment. Each impression we leave in the sand is the residue of our choice to take the next step. We cannot erase our footsteps, but we can learn and grow from them.

I learned a lot from my footsteps in the sand. I learned that we leave impressions wherever we go, not just in the sand. I learned that we leave impressions in people's hearts and minds by the way we treat them, by the choices we make and by the actions we take. I learned that we leave impressions in the environment through our decisions of what we consume and discard. I learned that we leave impressions on humanity by the legacy we leave when we die. I learned that we leave impressions everywhere. We can never erase a first impression but, if in examining our lives we don't like the impressions we are leaving, we can make a decision to move our life in a different direction. There is always a new path. There is always a new trail. There are always new options.

If you want to change the direction of your life, don't wait for a rock. And if one hits you, don't wait to be rescued. If you are ready to change your life, if you are ready to leave new impressions, dig deep inside your heart and use the courage you already have to examine your beliefs, to discard the beliefs that don't serve you anymore and to chart a new path. Chart that new path by looking beyond your current circumstances and conditions. What you see in front of you, the conditions of your life, is nothing more than the residue of your past. Don't focus on past effects. Focus on your new reality. Give energy to it and take action toward it. This takes emotional risk and courage. But life is risky and anything worthwhile involves risk. The risks don't seem big, though, when the change is something we truly desire.

Change is not always comfortable because past thoughts and beliefs will tug at our heart and mind, trying to pull us back to a place of certainty. But we always have a choice. We can play it safe or take risks. We can tiptoe into the oceans of life or we can take the chance to learn and grow by diving in and immersing ourselves in our full potential. We can walk on the sand to avoid the rocks and shells or we can be silly and playful and build sand castles. Each of these choices has its own outcome. The more risks we take, the more we are willing to let go of in order to move forward, the more courage, wisdom and personal strength we will gain. We all end up on the other side. We take nothing with us, but there is so much goodness to leave behind. If you look at your life right now, what sort of footprints will you leave behind?

There was so much more that I wanted to think about, but the afternoon was getting late, clouds were starting to form in the sky and a light drizzle was beginning to blow. It was time to turn around, return to the trailhead and bring closure to my day.

I stood up and, without continuing on to the place of my injury, paid homage to my rock and to mother earth for the incredible gift they gave me. I picked up a rock, held it tightly, closed my eyes and said a brief prayer of gratitude.

Great Spirit, thank you for the gift of this experience. Thank you for aligning my path with the falling rock and for all the transformation and blessings it has brought into my life. Thank you for the physical healing, the emotional healing and the spiritual healing. Most importantly, thank you for all the people who will be blessed through the lessons I have learned and shared.

As I opened my eyes, tears rolled down my face. I kissed the rock, pressed it to my heart, then tossed it in the direction of my collision with destiny. I placed a small bundle of sage on the foot of the trail and released myself from my past.

I remained mostly silent on my way back. I kept a hurried pace because desert rock can very slippery in the rain. I knew I had to stay ahead of the weather to avoid flash floods or other dangerous hiking conditions. As I hiked, one thought kept popping into my mind: How had I made it out of here with a head injury and a concussion? It was a hoof just trying to beat the weather. I can't imagine how I could have made it out with dehydration, loss of blood and a spinning head. That day truly was a miracle.

When I finally made it back to the top of the crack canyon, I again paused. The memory of arriving here on my day of injury flashed back into my head. An emotional knot built up in my belly like a quickly erupting volcano, and I again began crying. How had I made it out of here alive? I let my tears flow for a few minutes, then spoke another prayer of gratitude. After a few deep breaths, I regained my composure and began my climb down. When I reached the bottom of the trail, my eyes filled again. I fell to my knees, buried my head in my hands and, for several minutes, kept repeating Thank You...Thank You...Thank You.

A gentle breeze was blowing, and the drizzle was turning into a light rain. As my tears touched the ground tears of rain landed on my head. Mother nature was crying with me, tears of joy!

After a few minutes, the raindrops started tickling my bald head and I started laughing. I love the feeling of life. I love the feeling of raindrops on my skin because it means I'm alive. And what a gift that is!

I picked myself up, hurried back to my truck, cooled off in the air conditioning, munched organic grapes and strawberries and guzzled a bottle of water.

Then I switched on Richard Warner's solo bamboo-flute music, reentered the Chaco Canyon loop and began my drive back home to Telluride.

NINETEEN

Self - Love

You know you're in love when you can't fall asleep because reality is finally better than your dreams.
~ Dr Seuss

THROUGH MY JOURNEY of Footsteps After the Fall, I have come to see that we are the traveler and the trail, the seeker and the teacher. The experiences of life are the classroom, our thoughts are our map, and our heart is our guidance system. During this walk through life, we will dance many dances and accumulate the most marvelous collage of memories and emotions. Of the many things we accumulate during life's journey, there are only two things we leave behind: our relationships and our experiences. Both are predicated upon our relationship with our self.

Relationships form the foundation of life. There a relationship between the moon and the tides, between the sun and the wind, between the oceans and the rain, between the rivers and the streams, and between thoughts, emotions and things. Everything is connected to everything, and everything is interrelated. There is no escaping the interconnectedness of the universe.

The most important relationship we will ever have is the one we have with our own life. It's a relationship that is one of learning to be our own best friend and lover and of developing complete and untethered self-love.

Self-love is the dance and meditation of living in a place of total self-acceptance. We must love ourselves regardless of what we have gone through or of what is going on in the moment, without judgment or expectations, allowing our life to unfold into the effects of the natural flow of thoughts and emotions.

To love ourselves is to transcend the critical self and become our own biggest fan. It is to look in the mirror, regardless of our physical, mental, emotional, spiritual or financial condition, and accept ourselves as we are in that moment, unconditionally, knowing, at the same time, that we are always capable of a higher standard of life and self-worth.

To love ourselves is to give ourselves the gift of self-respect...to treat ourselves the way we would want others to treat us...to surround ourselves with quality friendships and relationships...to buy ourselves the gift flowers...to give ourselves the gifts that we would want others to give to us. To love ourselves is to take time to relax...to take care of our health...to pamper ourselves...to create the physical and emotional space to rest and rejuvenate...to move away from negativity and toward happiness...to do whatever makes us feel loved and happy in a healthy and meaningful way.

Once we have this type of authentic relationship with our life, we can have authentic relationships with others. We can reach out into other people's lives and have loving relationships with them because we will be reaching into their hearts with the intention of sharing our love, rather than seeing them as the source of our love.

Once we love our own life, we tap into an unlimited reservoir of energy that gives us the resources to have, do and be anything we want. Most importantly, the energy of love projects onto all of life and becomes a magnetic force for transforming the world. The energy of love is a contagious relationship between thoughts, emotions and things. Once we start walking with love in our heart, we will draw into our lives people of like heart and mind, and the power of love will grow and expand. Self-love is the seed, soil, water and sunshine to true happiness.

There is no greater experience in the world than to fall in love with our own life. Once we find the love that we seek within our own hearts, once we understand the laws of energy that shape our interactions with life, then the love that we find in own heart can be found in anyone's heart. When we love ourselves, we enter into a timeless state that allows us to see the love in everything, which is the ultimate reward of life.

There comes a time when you have to stand up and shout:
This is me damn it! I look the way I look, think the way I think, feel the way I feel, love the way I love! I am a whole complex package. Take me... or leave me. Accept me - or walk away! Do not try to make me feel like less of a person, just because I don't fit your idea of who I should be and don't try to change me to fit your mold. If I need to change, I alone will make that decision.
When you are strong enough to love yourself 100%, good and bad - you will be amazed at the opportunities that life presents you.
~ Stacey Charter

There is so much beauty and value to be found in learning the laws of life and the faculties of our mind. We have within our hearts and minds the tools to craft the reality of our choosing. The only restriction is time. Life will not go on forever. As eternal as a lifetime seems, its delicate canvas can end at any time, without warning. Once it ends, if we have not taken advantage of our full potential, we have missed out on the most magnificent gift imaginable.

The window of life is small. There is only one direction in life: forward. There is only one time in life: now. Regardless of how things appear in the moment, there is always a road ahead. There is always a new set of possibilities for the direction of our life. As long as we are moving forward, there will always be opened doors ahead. There are no closed doors, only closed hearts and minds. When one door appears to close, it is only because that experience no longer serves our higher good and it has given us a sign that we are ready to move in a different direction in life. If we are not living our life's purpose, doors will appear to close simply because they are guiding us to change direction. If we don't pay attention to the signs, those signs will become louder and louder, until we are "painfully ejected" and forced into a new direction...until rocks start to fall on our heads.

Let the experience of my rock be your guide. Pay attention to the signs that show up in your life. Pay attention to the pains, failures and setbacks. They are not there to harm you, but to guide you. If your approach to life is not working, if it does not feel right, or if your life seems to be falling apart, reach deep into the reservoir of your soul, grab onto the roots of your heart and mind and let go of the mental and emotional charade that is causing tidal waves in your journey.

Life is fragile, but it should not be feared. The only things we ever have to hold onto are the things we are afraid to let go of. Do not take this moment or this life, or anyone you love, for granted. Do not cling to the past. The past is nothing but an anchor that prevents you from sailing forward toward your dreams.

Allow your heart and mind to be free. Set your vision forward. With all your strengths and weaknesses, be excited about who you are and about the infinite possibilities life has to offer.

Learn to listen to your own thoughts. Learn how to think, to actually give thought to the potential outcomes of different choices. Learn how to make a decision, a true decision, where you take consistent action and don't judge circumstances by their appearances.

Learn how to listen to other people. Learn how to listen to their words and feelings. Learn how to be present when in the company of others.

Learn compassion - for yourself, for others and for nature.

Learn how to feel, to truly feel. Learn how to tap into the energy of emotions. There is true power in our emotions when they are self-guided, rather than when they are reactions to circumstances and appearances. How we feel gives energy, shape and form to the thoughts we are thinking. This is our reality.

Learn how to contribute. Learn how to love, to give without expectations or conditions. Contribute to the well-being of your friends, your family, your community and humanity. Give for the sake of giving. Not because you want something in return.

Learn how to find beauty and laughter in the moment. Learn how to move quickly from pain and sorrow to happiness and gratitude. Learn to trust that everything is happening by law. Therefore, learn how to live with lightness of heart, to not take people and life personally.

Learn how to communicate clearly and speak with integrity. Say only what you mean. Replace negative self-talk about yourself and others with words that will grow goodness, prosperity and community.

Lean how to say "no" to that which will weaken you, including your own self-limiting thoughts and beliefs. Learn to say "yes" to that which will give you inner-strength and self-respect.

Learn to think things through. Learn and understand that every choice has a result, a consequence.

Learn to be flexible — physically, mentally and emotionally.

Learn how to look at yourself and see your own beauty and potential. Learn how to harness that potential and turn it into your reality.

Learn how to be happy. Learn how to love yourself and to love others as an expression of that self-love.

Learn how to respect and take care of your own body, your mind, your temple. Learn how to eat properly, how to give your body the exercise it is hungry for.

Learn how to be self-reliant. Learn how to be a team player.

Learn how to surround yourself with positive, uplifting people who will encourage you and aid you in the pursuit of your dreams.

Learn how to understand and utilize the seven laws and the faculties of the mind. They are here to serve us, to help us move forward. The first step is always the most difficult. But once you open your mind to new possibilities and gain footing, once you create momentum, miracles will happen.

Learn to be authentic, to be your true-self, from the inside-out.

Lean to be at peace with life, with the moment and with the endless changes that come forth each day.

Take total responsibility for your life. Look back on your life experiences as lessons in a classroom. But this time, let it be up to you to decide which grade you receive, because you will decide the meaning you give to your experiences.

Do not relive your past, but learn from it. Gain a new perspective and make new, healthier choices for future actions.

Live with courage. Be honest and truthful, with yourself and others. Contribute to our world in a positive, meaningful way. Live from the heart. Live with passion. Live with purpose.

Honor those you love. Give your energy to that which creates beauty and gives light to life.

Above all, live in a place of laughter and gratitude.

TWENTY

Mirror of Truth

The unexamined life is not worth living.
~ *Socrates*

MY ENCOUNTER AT CHACO CANYON reintroduced me to the gift of life, that magical gift we receive from the angels of light when we are first born. The gift comes in a beautifully wrapped box and the Angels tell us that, with it, we can have, do and be anything we want. We are told that all the truth in the world, all the magic and power in the entire universe is contained within the gift and that we are to treasure, honor and respect it throughout our entire life.

Sadly, during the time of our first impressions of life, when we are introduced to the world, we forget about our gift. After we forget, it is as if our hearts, minds and imaginations have been blindfolded. We find ourselves going through life without any sense of purpose, awareness or direction. We want to feel loved and accepted. We want to feel significant, meaningful and connected. We want our dreams to come true. But somehow we become lost. We don't know where to go, what to believe or how to find our way. We seek everywhere for answers. We seek people, places, things, religions. We seek anything and everything we can find or imagine. Life seems unfair. We know what we want but we don't know how to get there. We are constantly bombarded with ideas, thoughts and beliefs. We are constantly bombarded with advertising images of who and what we should be. We find ourselves in a conflict between the known and the unknown, between our desires and our fears. We look at babies and see their beautiful innocence. Then we look at our lives and see complications. We desire success but we fear failure. We hunger for emotional freedom but we are slaves to conflicting thoughts and beliefs.

All we ever wanted was for our sandbox dreams to come true. All we ever wanted was the life of our dreams. Yet we look at our outside world and at the results showing up in our life, and we question our lives. Why were we given the opportunity to dream but never given an instruction book to make our dreams come true? Why do we have to play hide-and-go-seek with ourselves and others, with our own emotions, thoughts and beliefs? Why must we to pretend that it's okay to settle for less than our wildest dreams? Where did we learn to pretend, not like an imagining child but with an adult's fear and disillusionment? Where did we learn to replace creativity with distrust? We pretend everything is okay, but deep inside there is an emptiness, an unanswered question. We know something is missing. We don't know what it is. We just know it is gone.

It is the gift that is missing. It's not missing from us. We are missing from the gift. We are given an instruction book. But it's hidden within the gift of life. It has always been there.

When we were babies, we loved and cherished our gift. We kept it in our heart and mind. We loved the pretty wrapping paper, ribbons and bows. But we never opened it because we were mesmerized by its beauty. Since we never opened it, we never learned the truth of life. Instead, we fell into the hypnosis of life. We fell asleep and traded our gift and imagination for fear, and we entered the life of adulthood.

When I finally rediscovered my gift of life, it was nothing like what I had imagined or expected. It was something so obvious that it could not be easily seen. But it could be easily revealed. It was right in front of my face all the time but too far away to be recognized.

It's always there. Yet even if we are told of its existence, we do not see or understand it because we are too comfortable where we are. Life is funny that way. Just because we seek does not mean we will find. Desire is not what feeds us. Hunger is what feeds us. When we are truly hungry for answers, that is when truth begins to show up. Hunger does not come from desire. Hunger comes when we are empty, when we are vulnerable, when we are wanting because nothing else has worked. Hunger comes when rocks land on our head, when loved ones die, when we are injured, when we suffer a financial crisis, when we have hit bottom physically, mentally emotionally or spiritually. Our hunger is filled when we surrender to the possibility that there is more to life than we can possibly understand with our current level of awareness. Hunger is filled when we discover the true meaning of the gift of life.

A gift is never received until it is opened. When we are truly hungry is when we begin to ask questions again. That is when we look for the meaning of life, the gift of life. I was hungry. I was starving for answers. When I finally rediscovered my beautiful box, with the same eager anticipation of a young child receiving a birthday present, I untied the bows, tore off the wrapping paper, ripped the box opened and looked inside. I saw the unthinkable, the unimaginable and the impossible. I stared deeply into the gift. I became hypnotized by its simplicity. Could it be real? Had I gone through all of life looking for answers in all the wrong places? Had I lived my entire life backwards? I kept staring and staring and staring until I broke into hysterical laughter. I laughed so hard that I fell to the floor. My abs were aching from laughter. My eyes were tearing and my jowls were sore. I laughed from the depths of my heart and soul. I laughed all day and into the night.

> *Oh what a feeling to feel the feeling of a feeling set free.*
> *The bellyache of laughter,*
> *The sore jowls of joy.*
> *Oh what a feeling to laugh and feel joy!*

The gift of life is not life itself. Hidden within the box was everything I had ever looked for. All the answers to my questions were in plain sight.

Everything I had ever wanted and dreamed was right there. I had spent my entire life searching, seeking, wandering, questioning. It was all right there, and it had taken a rock to show me the truth.

There was nothing to take out of the box. Nothing! There was no book or scroll. No scriptures or letters. Nothing! The box was completely empty, but completely full. It was full of light. The box was a cube of mirrors. Inside and out, every side of the box was a mirror. When I looked into the box, I saw everything because it was then that I discovered the mirrors of truth. Life is a mirror. There is no truth outside our own heart and mind. Every experience in life is a mirror...a reflection of our own thoughts and beliefs. The gift of life is whatever we want it to be. It is up to us and our thoughts and imagination. Our imagination, combined with our five senses, the seven natural laws of the universe and the six faculties of our mind, are the tools for shaping and creating our experience of life.

The lesson from the hall of mirrors is real. It wasn't just a dream. We are all one people. All of life is connected. Life is an astonishing hall of mirrors, a collection of rainbow-colored reflections laid out like a mosaic, with each tile carrying its own story. The stories are stories about life, stories about the mystical laws that govern our relationship between thoughts, emotions and things.

There is no truth outside our hearts and minds. But there is plenty to explore. The laws of energy and the faculties of our mind give us the tools to paint our own reality. There are infinite realities to explore, infinite experiences to indulge in and infinite dances within the energetic matrix of life. Every face you see, every experience that you dance with, every moment you find yourself in is a mirror of truth. Our entire reality is shaped by the beliefs stored in our subconscious mind and made real through the seven laws of energy and the faculties of our mind. We live in a harmonic web of different realities, each reality reflecting a choice of destinies and each destiny a reflection of choices.

We are creative beings with unlimited potential. The experience of life is an ever-expanding story of inner reflection and outer expression. Every person on this planet is a unique expression of life and love. We each have our own strand of crystals that collects and reflects our thoughts, feelings and beliefs. Each crystal is a living entity that mirrors back to us the reflection of our consistent thoughts, feelings and beliefs. As we choose our thoughts and feelings, our crystal resonates the frequency that brings into reality a likeness of the images in our mind. Every choice that we make is a button that opens a window of opportunity. When the button is pushed and the window opens, we are given the choice to leap. From this leap, we gain the experience of our chosen reality.

The mirror of truth has been exposed. The hunt is over. There is nowhere to go. There is nothing to seek. There is no pill, person, place or thing than can make us feel more loved and more in love with life than the love we discover in our hearts. There is no guru or savior who can make us see the answers to our questions about who we are and what we are capable of. We can be shown truth through the written and spoken word. But seeing and understanding what we are shown only occurs when we open our eyes and are willing to learn. No one can open our eyes for us. No one can make us see. No one can make us look into the mirrors of truth. No one can make us understand the laws of energy and the power of the mind. The only time we see is when we are ready to see. Until then, life will show up each day as a reflection of the thoughts and beliefs that have been impregnated into our subconscious mind. And life will continue to seem like it is happening to us from the outside in rather than from the inside out, as a reflection of our own creation.

The laws of life are here to serve us. They are here to empower us, to give us the tools to shape our reality. They are here to give us the full experience of the gift of life and the gift of time. Learn to trust the laws. Have the courage to look at the results that have shown up in your life and take total responsibility for everything that you have experienced, touched and tasted. If you don't understand why things have happened, take responsibility for the meaning you give to the experiences. Create new first impressions by looking at life through the eyes of the seven laws. Observe the bouquet of life and realize that everything is possible. Let go of the fear and struggle of trying to do life, rather than be life. Learn to love yourself from the inside out. Learn to live from the inside out. Let go of any idea that you are a victim, that you are helpless.

Let the past be free. Garden your heart and mind. Pull out the weeds of fear, poverty, lack and limitation, and plant the seeds of your dreams — seeds of love, health, happiness, community, family, cooperation and endless prosperity.

Reclaim your personal power. Reclaim your imagination. Allow yourself to feel. Allow yourself to be loved and appreciated. Be the person you are looking for. Be the first person to say thank you. Be the first person to smile and laugh. Be the first person who shows up in other people's lives and makes a difference. Feed people's hearts and souls by focusing on their beauty, by sharing compliments freely. Focus on what is right and wonderful about this moment. Shift your focus to solutions. Feed the hungry of heart, mind, body and soul. Allow others the pleasure of giving. Receive by giving and give by receiving. Be a positive source of inspiration and encouragement. Contribute to the moment by turning on your heart and turning on your smile. Brighten the day by living in love. Everywhere you go, scatter seeds of gratitude and leave a legacy of big love.

When your magical end-of-life moment arrives, as it always does, remember to give thanks for the journey into the heart and mind of God. Leave this world with a smile and with seeds of your love and laughter having been scattered across the hearts of all the people you have met.

Life gave me exactly what I wanted. I was looking for answers and life knew that we can never find answers using the same level of awareness that created our questions. In order to learn something new, we have to grow.

Discovering the gift of life, the mirrors of truth, brought me onto the path of Giggle Yoga.

Giggle Yoga is the path of living life from the inside out. It is the journey of emotional and spiritual flexibility and total self-responsibility.

When we begin to live from the inside out, when we can look in the mirrors of life and take total responsibility for our life, when we can look past appearances and find the hidden treasure in all our experiences, when we can step back from our emotional entanglements and look in the mirror and laugh, then we have entered the path of the Giggle Warrior.

My personal rescue is over, but the journey has just begun.

Touch A Rock, Touch The Past.
Touch A Flower, Touch The Present.
Touch A Heart Eternity.

EPILOGUE:

The Ripple Effect

Love conquers all.
~Virgil

MY BEAUTIFUL SUNSHINE,
If the power of the ripple effect of all the love and beauty that you
share with the world could be painted with a picture, it would be the most
magnificent picture imaginable! It would be a picture of the summer sun
casting its light onto all of life.

The light would land upon the earth, illuminating everything that can
be seen, tasted, touched and smelled.

The light would penetrate the hearts, minds and bodies of all of life.
Every cell on earth would be filled with its radiance.

The light would dance through crystals and expand into the full
spectrum of the colors of a rainbow.

Each spectrum of color would send out beams of light and love,
casting into the world the healing power of color.

The colors would expand through all the flowers, trees, oceans, rivers
and streams, through all the animals, birds and insects. Everything on this
planet would bathe in the magical beauty of the healing power of color.

All the waters of the earth would be cleansed. The air would be purified and the earth would be restored to her natural purity. Hearts and minds would be cleansed and purified. Everything on earth would be healed and restored.

The air would be filled with the scent of the bouquet of every flower on earth. The waters of our world would splash in complete ecstasy, celebrating their own cleansing and purification.

Dolphins and whales would leap through the oceans in a playful dance of loving celebration, sending out joyful songs of peace, gratitude and harmony.

Birds and butterflies would sail through the skies. The smiles in their hearts would cast brilliant reflections onto the oceans and rivers, expanding the spirit of gratitude.

Elk and deer would sip the purified waters of the lakes and streams, launching an explosive burst of love from their hearts, as the waters cleansed from the colors of the rainbow nourished their bodies.

The entire earth would resonate a single tone of love and purity. That tone would blend with the colors of the rainbow and the sky would burst into a dancing celebration of light and song.

The song and dance would be a symphony of hearts sharing their gratitude for the gift of light.

All the earth — everything seen and unseen, everything living within her air, waters and upon her lands — would blend into a unified pulse of symphonic love and celebration.

The breath and pulse of light would return to its natural state of harmony. The air would be filled with rainbows. Angels would dance in the skies. The natural flow of giving and receiving would be restored.

The smiles of all the hearts of humanity and the love in the soul of every plant and animal would melt into an ocean of tears of gratitude.

Such is the power of the ripple effect of all the love that pours from your heart. You are a beautiful, charming, magnificent vessel of light and healing, leaving footprints of love everywhere you go.

Through the purity of your heart, you have blessed and transformed my life. What you are to me — a loving, gracious, tender, beacon of light — you are to all of life.

You are my Sunshine! Thank you for entering into my life. You have touched my heart in a way that I thought was only possible in my dreams. You are a dream come true!

All that I am — my heart, my mind, my soul and my life — is always open to your light...!

Namaste!

A Letter From Hawkwind

I received this letter from Hawkwind in 1985, while in College.

This Moment My Friend,
Not tomorrow or a year.

Emanate your love and wisdom in all you do.
From brushing your teeth to journeying the universe.

Live your life as you choose and above all:
Have Fun Always!

What you choose to give yourself to is all you're asking.

Pay attention to fear and destruction and you'll be drawn to it.

Pay attention to life and the creation of harmony and peace
and you will experience this – always.

Live your own dream. In your heart all is known.

Don't plan your life, live your plan.

Know who you are.
Love who you are.
Live the life that is you, in your heart.

Living high on Wilson Mesa amongst the hawks and winds.

Light Loves Life,
Hawkwind Soaring

Personal Poetry
Morsels From My Heart

Poetry is the music of the soul, and, above all, of great and feeling souls.
~ Voltaire

THROUGH THE PAST TWENTY-FOUR YEARS, poetry and writing has been my greatest tool for working through my thoughts and feelings, and clearing my heart and mind. Some people like to journal, I love to paint pictures with words.

Now that you have followed my journey of Footsteps After the Fall, I would like to offer you several of my writings as small morsels of love from the depths of my heart.

In appreciation for my second chance at life, I am honoring my father, Arthur Strauss, by including a short children's story that he wrote over forty years ago – Hibble Pibble and Zibble. He read it to me, my brother and sisters when we were children.

With Giggles, Love and Gratitude,
David Lloyd Strauss

...The Meaning of Life

From the deepest of seas, to the highest of peaks.

Through an unbelievable dance of emotion and adventure,
The meaning of life is finally revealed.

We are here, not for ourselves, but for each other.

We are here to partake in the full spectrum of human emotion,
and to journey the tastiest of journeys.

Life is about our senses...
About enjoying the moment.
Living all that can be lived.
Tasting all that can be tasted.

It is about the scent of flowers, and the color of a rose.

It is about the taste of chocolate
And the magical drool of a hot fudge sundae.

Life is about strawberries,
Hoola-hoops, birthday parties and Spaghetti O's.

Life is about water-skiing, mountain climbing,
Hiking, fishing and biking.

It is about the taste of pure water,
And the refreshing bubbles of your favorite soda.

It is about the cherry on the sundae, and the whip cream on nose.

Life is about the beauty of a lady-bug and the mystery of a moth.

Life is about the magic of a butterfly
and the scent of a rainbow painted sky.

Life is about the belly ache of laughter and tear drops of joy.
It is about the mosquito on the water and the frog atop the lily pad.

It is about stars, moons and clouds.

It is about root beer and ice cream,
Peanut butter and chocolate and Bavarian cream pie.

About loving ourselves and loving another.

It is a game of choices and a celebration of individuality.

From the first steps we take, to the last breath we breathe,
We are here to live, love and enjoy the full collage of the many faces,
Tastes and colors, of the magical world
Of the third planet from the sun.

It is here on earth that we are meant to live
And here on earth we are meant to expand our heart and mind
So that we can make real the wildest of imaginings.

We are meant to live freely with love...
To respect and honor this magical place.

Life is meant to be lived
And we are meant to laugh, love, and grow
With and amongst each other...
To taste the flavor of joy
And live the laughter of change.

We are and always will be
The flower in the garden
Of the mind of God.

David Lloyd Strauss
August 16th, 1996

169

...A Boy's Lost Mom

The emotional wheel
of time's hidden pain
Releases tears of an age-old child
Humbled by the passage
of time's hurtful gain.

Tears in belly, tears in heart
Tears in eyes.

Tears of yesteryear's pain
Finds release in the song
Of a boy's lost mom.

From days of youth
to days of today
The tear-filled child
Finds lament over the pains
Of yester-years emotion.

Strong has he been
In his quest to be free
But in hiding his pain
He has lost that magical flame
Which keeps a growing child
Happy and free.

Yet through this song
A song about mom
A reservoir of hidden tears
Cascades from his heart
Creating a wonderful story
Of surrender and psalm.

As tears fall to the ground
Pillow and cloth in arm
The energies of love find
expression
Through the freedom release

Of emotion unharmed.

Indeed, the child's lost mom
Was a source of great pain.

But more pain has there been
In trying to be strong.
For in the strength
of hidden emotion
The pain of an eternity
Congests the child's heart
Eclipsing his love
As a moon to the sun.

No more he cries! No more!
No more shall he eclipse his heart
And hide the humanity
That makes him real.

Whether it be tears of joy
Or dew-drops of sorrow.
I am the age-old child.

I am free to love, free to live
And free to shed and share
The feelings
That make the man in me
Eternally happy
And graciously free.

In full surrender
I remain
Calmly yours,

David Lloyd Strauss
December 16th, 1999

...Chimes of Love

In the chamber of our heart
Resonates the mystical
song of love.

As flutes of faith
Dance with chimes of love
The true mystery of life
Unfolds into a rainbow of colors
Carefully cast upon
The play-write of our heart.

As the colors of truth merge
Into a crossroads of dreams
The mirrors of light
Find their home
In the patterns
Of our dreams.

Through the tapestry of time
The thoughts of
Imagination and dreams
Have danced across our minds
And now mirror themselves
Into the reality we are seeking.

A reality painted with the colors
Of light and sunshine
Dancing across the palate
of our hearts
And the tapestry of time.

As the painting unfolds
The image of our thoughts
Begin their dance
of physical form.
In this dance

The artistic images
of the prisms of love
Are forever set-free
So that the truth of life
May be shared
And revealed to all.

The artistic dance of life
Is a contagious celebration
Of the beauty
Of the family
Of
"we".

We are each
The sculptor and the sculpture
The painter and the painting.

We are the palate of colors
The tapestry, the brush
And the creative mind
Singing through
The heart of eternity.

Loving and sharing
The uniqueness
Of our humanity.

We are all welcomed
Because we are all free.

We are free
Because
We are love!

David Lloyd Strauss
July 25th, 1995

...Celebration of Life

The dance of birth.
The pinnacle of creativity.

Awaken my child
Awaken to the glory of the garden.

Open thine eyes and see in your heart
The palate of colors
As a smorgasbord of realities.

Each stroke of creation
Celebrates
The charm and glory
Of God's ever-blossoming
Prism of love.

This earth
This planet
It is our home.

It is the magical garden
In the bountiful painting of life.

Come home.
Come home my dear ones.

Return to the eternal mystery
And magic of life.

David Lloyd Strauss
March 31st, 1994

...A World of Darkness

The marching tides of death.
The transparency of emotion.

That lost feeling that I once was
And today am not.

The self that was stolen.
The pride that was eaten.
The esteem that was crushed.

What is it in the life of a being
That gives permission to steal
The essence of humanity?

What of all this pain?
Why do we go through it?

Some say this is a world
of darkness.
That all we do has no meaning
But to suffer and wallow
in sin original.

More there is
and I see it now.
To live in the kingdom
Is where I want
To be.

To walk amongst the birds,
Chipmunks, lions and bears.

To be at peace
with moments gone by.

To enjoy the tranquility
Of the pulse of time.

On and off.
Up and down.
It is always today.
And the tomorrow's
that we dream about
They are made real
By the thoughts and will
Of the choices of today.

Calmness and serenity.
Laughter and joy.

The dance of emotion
Is fueled through
Acceptance of change.

Amidst the kingdom
We walk about
With fortitude and strength
Knowing who we are
And who we serve.

The life of yesterday
It may have hurt
It may have harmed.
But is it today?

Why do we carry with us
The shackles of our past
And encage ourselves
In the prison of emotion?

Across the tides of time.
Behind facades of joy
And mirrors of smiles,
Hide our fears of pain
And emotions of worry.

As our wounds of time
Turn into scars of pain
Our scars turn into walls
And our walls into prisons.

Within this prison
Our Pandora's box
We create the perfect
Place of hiding.
A place of protection
Where walls are built from fears.
The shackle and chain
Links of "I can't".

And the prison door
Words of criticism and ridicule
Spoken by others
Believed by us.

Some of us have windows.
Some do not.

But until we crumble these walls
And free our past
We will pace this prison
With the ferocity
Of a cat in a cage
Circling about,
Restrained from reality
Without goal or meaning.

Face death we must.

The mirror of our past
Must become the reason
To crush our fears.

Do it now I say…
And allow these walls
To crumble
To the ground.

David Lloyd Strauss
March 30th, 1994

174

...Fruit of Innocence

Through a journey of
lost emotions
To a land of broken promises.

By way of a roller coaster
of adventure
And a collage of
uncertain destinies
What once seemed impossible
I now see as real.

And the reality I see
Is the expansion of truth
Through the mirror of my life.

The truth of laughter
The truth of light -
The truth of life.

The truth of love
expanding its beauty
Through my heart to yours.

Through a collision of destinies
And a pasture watered with tears.

In a moment of surrender
Where my spirit was broken
I followed the instincts
of my heart

And leaped from my nest of fear
Into the garden of God.

Knowing that though this
transition appeared to be a
dark and ugly cave
What I was leaping into
Was the gentle grace
Of the invisible hand of Love.

A hand hidden In the
abyss of faith
Only to be seen by those
special people
Who choose to be free.

Through my surrender and leap
What seemed like a death
was in fact
A new beginning to my life.

And this magical beginning
has begun
And through grace
has it started.

To that which I was once
attached I have now let go.

And with whom I was once
angry I now have forgiven.

And more than anyone else
It was myself
that I never
forgave.

But now having done so
I am free to be me.

And in becoming free
I have discovered a life filled
With the innocence of dreams

And in these dreams I am amidst

A playground of friends
A collage of personalities
Who have also chosen to be free.

In what seems like a flash in time
A moment in God's mind
What I have always been
searching for
I have finally
found.

That quiet place in my heart
That I can safely call home.

David Lloyd Strauss
March 24th, 1996

...Garden Child of Justice

A taste of the real
is the flavor we seek.

A sensation of realities governing
the memories
of truths once
forgotten.

The trail of illusions
from times now past
Solidifies the stories
of yesteryears gone by.

The shackles of memory
serve no more
For it is here now
that our truths belong.

To live the life consistent with
who I am
And turn the taste of truth
Into a salad of realities.

To live and enjoy the family of all
And live the life
of the fullness of dreams.

Begin now
The heart-song dance
of naked love.

Chant the holy chant
Cries the community of love.

Return to the living presence
Of surrendered realities
and begin walking
The passionate testimony
of garden truth.

Live the piercing brilliance
of heavenly light
And seek no more that which is
Already known
but sing from the heart
And be who we are.

The light, the love, the truth.

The garden child of justice.

The heart-song celebration
Of testimonial realities.

Dance the blissful dance of change
and be the one truth
which governs
our reality.

That we, you and I.
The flowers, the trees
the rocks and stones.

The animals of land and sea.
Birds of air and soil.
Insects and bugs.
Organisms of air, water and fire.

Each of us, together as one family
We are the purity of love
And mirrors of life.

We are the mystery and magic
Of God's eternal
community of grace.

We are here to fulfill our
destiny of devotion.
To return home and restore
the hidden heavens
and bountiful gardens
of light, love,
justice and truth.

We...
Together as one thread of life

We are the breath and pulse of life
Re-birthing
from a millennium
of
change.

We are earth
and earth is our home.

Welcome again
to the truth of we
For there is none other.

May we all return with god-speed
To the inner-thread of Light.

~ David Lloyd Strauss
September 20th, 1994

178

...Who We Are

We are sculptors. Our body, mind and life, our sculpture.

Our tools are love, honesty, patience, compassion,
Attentiveness, sincerity, quietude, humor and tears.
All of which, when combined, create the perfect expression of life.

Who we are, the image we hold of ourselves, is the sum of our thoughts
and beliefs about our self and personality, and is only as attractive
as we perceive it and create it to be.

Who we are, our life, is simply the pulse of thought, action and inaction.
And the dance of emotions is as much a natural part of our existence
As is the setting of the sun and changing of the tides.

With the changing tides of life,
To have love for our self and another is also the intended course of life.
And, loving another and one another matters not if it is man or woman.
Rather, it is the impetus to be with another, to care, support, encourage
And be truthful that unites the flame of humanity.

In some moments of time there is great action, in others, stillness.
Yet even amidst stillness, life continues its pulse.

It is with action however, and the courage to move forward
that we become a part of the tidal waves of growth
through the changing currents of experience.

It is said that extraordinary stories come from people
who have chosen to be extra-ordinary.
From people who have taken the chance
to stretch and extend beyond the bounds of fear and uncertainty,
into the realms of spirit, beyond mundane thought and expression.

Those that choose to be guided by the laws of love will find themselves in
an ocean of abundance, mercy, grace, compassion and fulfillment.

It is not the behavior of love, but the choice to be, to mirror and to reflect
the way of love that brings us into the true path of life,
what some call, the path of the heart.

Anger and hatred, as much as they are feared and avoided,
Are as much a part of love as are grace, mercy and compassion.

The human experience then is not one of constant joy and serenity,
But rather a dance of honesty of emotions and feelings.

The simplicity is then revealed.
Seek we not first honesty with others, but with ourselves,
For by being true to ourselves, we fortify our will to be honest with others.

The greatest bearers of non-truth are the fears we hold onto
which create the walls that shelter us from who we truly are.
And these walls are the barriers
which hold us back from our truest potential.

It is not what we have done in times past that burdens our soul,
but that which we hold onto and carry with us
that acts as the ball and shackle against freedom and change.

True freedom then is not only our ability
to say "yes" to that which we want.
But also the ability to say "no" and move away from those experiences
which may lead us away from the truth of our heart.

True freedom comes in time with the commitment to flexibility in character
and belief, and through a heart that is willing to learn and grow.

With true freedom comes true love.
And the truth of true love, as simple as it is, can seem deeply hidden.

True love is not something sought outwardly,
but rather sought and found within
The aspirations of friendly, honest relations with one's own self.
Life is the opportunity to learn to love ourselves
and to express that love by loving others.

Loving our self and another
is the greatest expression of our freedom.

~ *David Lloyd Strauss*
October 19th, 1998

...Sandbox Dreams

MANY YEARS AGO there stood a child in the sun, gleefully dreaming about the life he was about to live. It was a beautiful summer morning. The heat of the sun warmed the cool dawn air. Chipmunks wrestled in the trees and song birds sang with the gaiety of new born life. Flowers blossomed, painting the air with their magical scent and colors...creating the backdrop for a mystical day of dreaming.

All was calm. The sunlit tree-tops cast images of their branches across the waters below. The dance of shadows amidst the throws of light gave a sense of vibrancy to the stillness of the moment. In the background echoed the cheers of children, as they danced amongst the butterflies and bees. Pogo-sticks, hoola-hoops, GI-Joes, Barbies and match-box cars littered the ground in a feeding frenzy of fun. As the children danced from game to game, they played with each other with the innocence of new born life. From sand-box to slide, swing to jungle-gym, each of the children explored their imaginations, expanding their dreams into the horizons of their minds.

The colors of the day fashioned a scene that only a child could see through an untainted imagination. And for this one child...the child in the sun...the child about to dream, this child was special. His dreams were not ones of things. But of things created with love. It was his dream to always have a home...a place to return to...a place to be nurtured...a place to be free. The things he saw were things of beauty. A beautiful home nestled amidst a forest of trees and garden of flowers. A place were birds sang freely and the elk and deer could safely roam. A place where friends could play...where the food was always yummy, clothes always clean, and love always shared.

The child was young and knew no limits. As he imagined this home, he imagined the most magical of dreams. His home was a Castle...draw-bridge and all, keenly decorated with the colorful scent of limitless thinking. From his mind could he see, and through his heart did he paint...painting a picture of a life destined to be loved, accepted and free.

With the sun beating upon his hide, matchbox car in hand, he built his Castle out of sand, knowing that one day it would become real. Using sea-shells as windows, sticks as flag poles and stones as doors. As his mind expanded, his castle grew...soon gaining a barn and stable, filled with cattle, sheep and horses. His horses gained a corral and the corral a passage way to the mountains. In the mountains he saw himself riding briskly through the trees...splashing along the river...cooling in the shade of stone. Waterfalls became rivers. Rivers became streams. Streams became ponds and ponds, places of quietude where a resting soul could reflect upon the life he was destined to live.

Back at the castle, toys were scattered about. Ferrari's, Lamborghini's, Porsche's, Speed Boats, Airplanes and Motorcycles - every matchbox of his dreams was neatly organized in a place which one day he would call home.

As the child played in the sand, a halo of happiness surrounded his being. He knew that if it weren't for his dreams, he would have no castle. If it weren't for his imagination, he would have no place to call home.

...Hibble Pibble and Zibble

By Arthur M. Strauss

A Children's Story About 3 Frogs
Hibble – Pibble –Zibble

This children's story was written by my Father, Arthur Strauss, over forty years ago. He read it to me, my brother and sisters when we were children. It has never been published. To honor his creativity, and his loving, caring heart, I proudly share it here.

A SIGN ON THE BULLETIN BOARD in the town of Tibble announced a jitterhop dance to be held in the neighboring town of Jibble. Three frogs, named Hibble, Pibble and Zibble, who lived in the town of Tibble, decided to go to the jitterhop dance in the town of Jibble. They always hopped together no matter where they went, and always hopped in this order: Hibble hopping to the left, Pibble hopping in the front, and Zibble hopping to the right. This is the way they hopped to the town of Jibble.

On the way to the town of Jibble, Hibble Pibble and Zibble decided to take a shortcut through the woods. These woods were no ordinary woods. They were home to the fairy frog Libble, who lived on her lily pad in the pond. They proceeded to hop through the woods, Hibble hopping to the left, Pibble hopping to the front and Zibble hopping to the right. This shortcut, through the woods where the fairy frog Libble lived on her lily pad, was always deserted. No one ever used it because there was a legend that the fairy frog Libble, who lived on her lily pad in the pond, would cast a spell on anyone she caught on the path. The woods were shroud in mystery. No one had ever met the fairy frog or knew what the spell might

183

be. But Hibble, Pibble and Zibble were close friends. They were very adventurous and were sure that they would be able to take care of themselves.. The real reason for taking the shortcut was that they didn't believe in legends.

It was a very bright day and the sun shining through the trees had cast strange shadows in the woods where Hibble, Pibble and Zibble were hopping towards the town of Jibble on their way to the jitterhop dance. The frogs were very frightened, for the shadows seemed to move as the trees swayed in the gentle wind. It was also strangely quiet in the woods. Hibble, who hopped to the left, Pibble, who hopped to the front, and Zibble, who hopped to the right, might have enjoyed their hopping very happily in the hot humid forest , except for the shadows that always changed shape as the gentle wind swayed through the trees. Sometimes the shadows looked as huge as flying reptiles that seemed to swoop down on Hibble, Pibble, and Zibble to carry them off. At other times, the shadows seemed like dancing puppets jiggling up and down to the tune of the puppeteer's music. But the strangest shadow of them all looked like a huge scaly serpent that seemed to open its jaws in the attempt to swallow up Hibble, Pibble and Zibble. At the very moment that the scaly serpent was about to swallow up Hibble, Pibble, and Zibble, a huge black cloud appeared and blotted out the sun. The forest became dark as night. There were no more shadows — just one big sheet of darkness. It was so dark that Hibble, Pibble and Zibble couldn't see where they were hopping. Hibble hopped to the left and hopped into a tree. Pibble hopped to the front and hopped into the water. Zibble hopped to the right and hopped into a rock.

The darkness lasted for one hour and everything on the forest path stood still. The trees stopped rustling in the wind. The animal noises disappeared, the crickets stopped chirping, and the cold air settled across the entire forest. The only thing that came to life was the bats, who swarmed everywhere. Hibble and Zibble just lay on the fern floor of the forest. Pibble who landed in the water floated around, keeping very still. Suddenly, the cloud moved away, as quickly as it appeared. The bats disappeared. The sun shined again through the trees, once more casting eerie shadows on the path through the woods where Hibble, Pibble and Zibble had hopped toward the town of Jibble to go to the jitterhop dance.

During this blackout, Hibble, Pibble, and Zibble had been completely stunned. Their minds had gone blank. Hibble, who had hopped to the left and hit a tree had a huge bump on his head. Pibble, who'd hopped to the front and into the water, was nowhere to be seen. And Zibble, who'd hopped to the right and hit a rock, had a huge bump on his nose. Hibble and Zibble became terribly frightened. What had happened to Pibble? The sun shining through the trees caused such strange shadows over the water that Hibble and Zibble didn't see the dark water in front of them. Oddly, this happened to be the pond where the fairy frog Libble lived on her lily pad.

Hibble looked at Zibble and saw the bump on his nose. Zibble looked at Hibble and saw the bump on his head. Hibble didn't look like Hibble to Zibble and Zibble didn't look like Zibble to Hibble. They both looked like different frogs to each other. They forgot their worry about Pibble. They stared at one another, Hibble to Zibble and Zibble to Hibble. They realized how funny they looked with their bumps and they began to laugh and laugh and laugh and laugh and laugh. They laughed so hard and so long that they laughed themselves to sleep on the fern floor of the forest.

Meanwhile, Pibble was in trouble. It so happened that on this specific day, Libble the fairy frog, had cast a spell on the path through the forest that led to the town of Jibble. It was written in the clouds that once a year the fairy frog Libble shall cast a spell on this path that would darken the way for any strangers journeying to Jibble. Once this spell was cast, the powers of the fairy frog Libble would be preserved for one more year, and anyone falling into the pond would come under the magic spell of Libble the fairy frog. Thus, when Pibble fell into the pond, he was cast under the spell of Libble the fairy frog.

Libble was delighted. For many years, she had tried so hard to lure frogs into the pond, but no frogs had been on the path during the magic spells. This time, she'd actually caught one. It was written in the clouds that the only way a spell could be broken was for the pond to run dry. When the ponds ran dry, the fairy frog Libble would lose her powers, and she would turn into an ordinary frog.

In the meantime, Hibble and Zibble, who had fallen asleep on the fern floor of the forest, were hidden by the strange shadows cast by the sun through the trees. Libble the fairy frog could not see them, and she did not know they were there. She was so happy to have the company of Pibble, who was under her spell, that her thoughts did not go beyond the waters of the pond.

Libble was a very lonely frog. She lived all alone on her lily pad in the pond. She never saw any other frogs. Everyone was afraid of the legend they heard of being cast under her magic spell. The legend was carried by the winds that whispered softly into their ears. Everyone believed in the whispers of the wind. Only Hibble, Pibble, and Zibble didn't believe what the wind whispered to them. The wind listened and knew everything. It sent messages all over the land. Those who didn't heed the wind's whispers scoffed at them as mere rumors, which is what Hibble, Pibble, and Zibble did. They called these whispers silly rumors, which certainly annoyed the wind. So as Hibble, Pibble, and Zibble started to hop through the forest shortcut to the jitterhop dance, the wind heard of their journey and carried news of it through the forest to Libble the fairy frog who lived on her lily pad. Libble believed in the whispers of the wind, and so she cast her spell, and now Hibble, Pibble, and Zibble were really in trouble.

It took a while for Pibble to realize that something was wrong. He'd jumped into the pond when darkness fell on the forest path, and at first he enjoyed the nice, cool water, because the path had been hot. He paddled around happily while Libble perched on her lily pad and observed him carefully. But then, Pibble suddenly realized that his two friends, Hibble and Zibble, were nowhere to be found. He became quite worried and decided to get out of the pond to look for them. He swam to the shore. As soon as he tried to get out, he slid right back into the pond. He tried again…and again, but each time that he reached the shoreline, he slid back into the pond. Pibble was trapped in the pond because of the magic spell of Libble the fairy frog. At first, Pibble thought that he was falling back into the pond because the sand was very loose and gave way under his weight. He tried another part of the pond, but the same thing happened again, and he slid back into the water. Pibble, who was starting to become frantic, tried to get out at several other places, and each time, he slid back into the water.

Libble the fairy frog did not know that her spell could be broken if the pond ran dry. She only knew that her happiness as a fairy frog depended on having a frog under her spell — a frog that would share with her the magical world of lily pads on the pond, and the magical waters of the pond itself. Libble the fairy frog did not know of any other world except the pond. When Libble was only a tadpole swimming around this pond, a magical cloud appeared and darkened the forest. It spewed forth torrents of rain so hard that the pond overflowed and washed away every living thing, except Libble, the tiny tadpole who was caught between two rocks. When the rain stopped, the magical cloud left some of its magic in the waters of the pond. The pond became enchanted and trapped all living things within its banks. The only living thing was Libble, the tiny tadpole. The magical spell was such that if any living thing tried to get out of the pond, it would automatically slide back into the water. The magical waters were such that those who lived in them were to live forever.

The magic could not go beyond the pond. When Libble outgrew being a tadpole and became a full grown frog, she tried to get out of the pond, but each time she tried, she slid back in to the water. She finally accepted the fact that she would never be able to leave the pond. Because Libble lived alone on the lily pad in the pond, she became sensitive to the ways of nature, especially the wind. She always listened to the whispers of the wind, which carried tales from faraway places, and she believed in the tales. It is from listening to the whispers of the wind that Libble knew of other frogs, and it is how other frogs knew of the magic spell that was cast over the pond.

Pibble was trapped in the pond, and when he saw Libble sitting on her lily pad, he swam over to her and climbed onto an adjoining lily pad. He was so happy to see another frog that he completely forgot about Hibble and Zibble. Libble was also very happy to see a real live frog (Pibble). She had heard about other frogs by listening to the whispers of the wind, but this was the first time she had ever seen a frog. They were both very delighted with each other and they began to swim around the pond. They swam underwater, hopped on lily pads, dived off of logs, and frolicked around as gleefully as could be. They played for hours and even invented a few new games. Libble would sit on a lily pad and Pibble would grab the lily pad and pull it around the pond, then he would try to pull it underwater to dunk Libble. But each time Libble saw Pibble go underwater, she would hop to another lily pad, and Pibble would pull down an empty lily pad. Pibble became very frustrated whenever Libble hopped to another pad, so he tried to outfox Libble. He would swim underwater to the other end of the pond and lift his head up alongside a log to see where Libble sat. Then, he would swim towards her underwater, get beneath her lily pad and tilt the pad so Libble would topple off into the water. Libble became very upset whenever Pibble fooled her this way. It was new for Libble to experience any kind of a feeling. She never saw or played with another frog before she met Pibble — as a result she never experienced any feelings. But now she was experiencing all different kinds of feelings.. She was experiencing anger, frustration, love and happiness. She began to feel like a complete frog.

Libble stared at her reflection in the water. Pibble, seeing her stare at her reflection, swam underwater and poked his head up through the reflection to stick his tongue out at Libble. For a moment Libble was astounded. She thought her eyes were playing tricks on her, she thought it was her own reflection, be she didn't know she had stuck out her own tongue. She rolled her tongue around to see if it was still in her mouth. It was still inside. Then, slowly, she stuck out her tongue keeping her eyes on what she thought was a reflection of herself in the water. Pibble seeing her stick out her tongue began to slowly put his tongue back in his mouth. Libble was staring at the face of Pibble with no tongue sticking out, and she became very frustrated and her green skin turned pink. Pibble began to laugh when he saw how pink Libble looked. Libble then realized that Pibble had played a joke on her, and she turned back to her natural shade of green, and, like a good sport, began to laugh. Libble was as happy as can be and Pibble was enjoying himself too, but not as much as if his friends Hibble and Zibble had been there. He missed them very much. Every time he thought of them, he swam to the shore and tried to get out, but each time he tried, he slid back into the pond. He asked Libble to help him get out, but Libble told him that he could never get out, and that the pond was his new world. Pibble suddenly realized that Libble was the fairy frog that he had heard about from the whispers of the wind. Libble looked at Pibble, and saw from the expression on his face, that Pibble knew she was the fairy frog.

Meanwhile, Hibble and Zibble, who had laughed themselves to sleep on the fern floor of the forest, began to wake up. First Hibble moved. He reached up, then stretched his legs, raised his head and saw that his friend Zibble still asleep. Hibble reached out with his leg and began to tickle Zibble with his toe. Zibble jumped up, frightened, and landed on Hibble's stomach. Hibble didn't realize this was an accident, so he grabbed Zibble's leg and toppled him over his head. Zibble flipped over and, on purpose, he landed on Hibble's stomach again. Soon they were fighting with each other, jumping, flipping, tickling, slapping and slipping on the fern floor of the forest. After about ten minutes of this nonsense, they both sat down, exhausted and covered with mud. Zibble remarked to Hibble how silly they had been to waste all this time fighting when they should have been looking for their friend Pibble. Hibble agreed. They shook hands, made up and decided to find Pibble.

Some time ago, when Hibble, Pibble and Zibble first became friends, they worked out several plans to help each other in case they became separated or lost. The first plan was to sit still and croak out the name of the friend who was lost. They would do this for about fifteen minutes in the hope that the lost frog would hear their croaks and follow the sound to its origin. The second plan was for one frog to sit still while the other frog hopped around him in a circle ten feet in diameter. Then, the frog who was hopping would stop and sit still while the other frog would hop around him in a circle ten feet apart and ten feet away in another direction. They would continue to do this to cover a large territory in the hope of finding the lost frog. They decided to try their first plan. They began croaking together very loudly, and after a few minutes they became exhausted, so they stopped. They decided that croaking together was not such a good idea. They felt that if one of them croaked at a time it would give the other a chance to rest.. They each began to croak one at a time very loudly – so loudly in fact – that the wind refused to carry their sound. They didn't realize that they had to whisper for the wind to be able to carry their croaks to the pond where their friend Pibble was trapped. Their croaking brought no results, so they decided to try their second plan. Hibble stood still while Zibble hopped around him ten feet away in a circle. When it came time for Hibble to hop around Zibble, Zibble stopped in the opposite direction of the pond without even realizing it. They hopped around each other, getting further and further away from the pond. After hopping around each other for almost an hour, in the opposite direction of the pond, they decided to stop and rest before figuring out how they would find Pibble.

Back at the pond, when Pibble realized that Libble was the fairy frog, he knew he was doomed, even though he could live forever in these magical waters. His world was greater than that of the pond. He had lived in cities and towns, and he had traveled far and wide. He enjoyed meeting other frogs and seeing new places. He enjoyed parties, dances and picnics. He knew he would become bored living within the confines of the pond. For Libble it was different. She only knew the world of the pond, and now that she had someone to share it with. She was very happy.

Pibble's joy from playing in the pond all but disappeared. Libble looked at Pibble and saw how unhappy he looked. She immediately became unhappy, another feeling that she had never experienced. Pibble felt his whole world closing in on him. His mind flashed back to the freedom he had before he landed in the pond, and he became very angry with Libble for trapping him. Libble looked at Pibble, and she felt his anger towards her and she began to cry. She told Pibble how selfish he was to think only of himself and his freedom when she never had any freedom and had never seen another frog. She tearfully told Pibble how happy she had been to frolic with him, and, for the first time in her life, she was experiencing different feelings. She also told Pibble that she knew he heard the whispers of the wind that told about the fairy frog and that any frog getting into the path could fall under a magic spell. But, he ignored these whispers as silly rumors, and he came to the forest on his own free will. She told him how wonderful she felt about him after he had given her a new outlook on life. Her crying and her expression of how she felt were so real that Pibble forgot his anger and showed Libble generous warmth and understanding. He realized it was useless to stay angry, and besides, he was really beginning to like Libble. Even though he knew that the magical waters of the pond would always hold him prisoner and never allow him to play with his friends, he would try to adjust to being alone with her and enjoy the pond.

The wind had been blowing gently all day and the whispers of the wind carried Pibble's conversation with Libble through the forest to where

Hibble and Zibble were. At first Hibble and Zibble thought they were imagining things, but they were willing to follow any clue that would lead them to their Pibble. After hearing the whispers of the wind they realized their friends was under the spell of the fairy frog in her pond. The whispers, which they were now ready to believe, were similar to the whispers they'd heard before- the whispers they had called silly rumors. Hibble held up a leaf to see which way the wind was blowing. It was blowing from the opposite direction they were heading. They both turned around and began hopping down the forest path toward the wind to rescue Pibble from the magic spell of the fairy frog Libble.

It was a bright day and the sun shining through the trees cast strange shadows on the fern floor of the forest. Hibble and Zibble, who have been so afraid before, were not even aware of the shadows now. Their only thought was to get to Pibble as quickly as possible. Hopping quickly on the forest path, Hibble and Zibble came upon the path where they each had bumped their head and nose. They stopped, sat down, and listened to see if they could hear any sounds that would guide them to Pibble. They heard splashing sounds that came from a cluster of bushes half hidden by the shadows of the trees.

They crept towards an opening in bushes, and they saw the pond in front of them. They stopped immediately and remembered that they had heard from the whispers of the wind that Pibble was trapped in the magical waters of the pond. They knew that if they went into the pond to help him, they would be trapped too. They looked around the pond from the shoreline and followed the noise of the splashes. There they saw Pibble playing with another frog. They were hopping on and off of the lily pads into the water.

Hibble and Zibble both began croaking. Pibble heard these familiar sounds and became so excited that he forgot all about his new friend Libble. He swam to the opposite side of the pond to where his friends Hibble and Zibble were calling him. Libble became a little annoyed at Pibble for leaving her in the middle of their game, but when she saw the two other frogs, she became excited too and swam over toward them. She asked them to hop in the pond and join Pibble and herself in a frolic. Pibble warned them not to, or they would be trapped forever, just like he was.

Pibble tried to climb out of the pond, and each time he slid right back into the magical waters. Then, Hibble and Zibble had an idea. Maybe if they held a stick over the water, Pibble could grab it, and they could haul him ashore.

They tried and tried, but it just didn't work. Pibble could not hold onto the stick, his hands kept slipping off. As long as he was in the magical waters of the pond he couldn't get out. Hibble and Zibble were quite upset about not being able to rescue him. So near and yet so far. They threw the stick away and began to walk around the pond to think of other plans to rescue Pibble.

Back in the pond, Libble was very excited to have seen other frogs. She asked Pibble if there were many more frogs beyond the waters of the pond. Pibble explained to Libble that there were thousands upon thousands of frogs who lived in cities, towns, villages and hamlets, each with their own array of ponds. Libble felt herself getting very excited. She wanted to learn what kind of life the frogs in the outside world lived, how they played and everything else about them. It would be such an adventure.

Pibble felt her excitement and he also knew that Libble secretly wanted to live in the outside world. Pibble didn't know how to describe it to her, so he decided the place to start was with himself and his friends, Hibble and Zibble. He told Libble how he, Hibble and Zibble had been on their way to the town of Jibble to a jitterhop dance. He told all the details of the dance, about the band, their instruments, and he even hummed a little tune, of the most popular songs. He told Libble about the dance contest where the best jitterhopper would get a door prize. He showed her how to do the jitterhop dance, and Libble loved it. She asked Pibble to dance some more and to teach her the breaks, dips, flops, hops, turns, twists, tumbles and spills. Pibble was very happy to teach Libble the dances, since he loved to dance and was an excellent dancer.

Pibble's first attempt to teach Libble started out by his telling her an imaginary tune so she could get a rhythm and a beat of a dance step. Pibble hummed a tune several times, then he asked Libble to hum it. She tried but she became very confused as she was halfway through the tune. Pibble was extremely sensitive to Libble, and he was very patient with her. He realized that the only way for Libble to learn was for him to teach her very slowly, not to rush her, to correct her mistakes with understanding, and not to get angry with her if she didn't catch on very quickly. After a while, under the patient tutelage of Pibble, Libble got the essence of the rhythm of the song and she was able to hum it quite well.

Pibble was very pleased at the way Libble picked up the tune, and he proceeded to teach her the jitterhop dance. They hopped onto the lily pads. Pibble held Libble's waist with his right hand and with his left hand he held her right hand. They began to hum the tune together to establish the rhythm of the dance. Then Pibble began dancing the steps with Libble. Hopping, twirling, breaking, dipping, flipping, turning, twisting, tumbling and spinning. Libble had natural rhythm, and she picked up the steps very quickly. Her excitement also helped her put an extra bounce in her steps that made the dance seem more lively. Pibble was amazed at how quickly Libble picked up the steps. He felt she was a natural dancer. He knew the only thing Libble needed was practice.

Pibble was so confident of Libble's ability that he decided to teach her more difficult dance steps. They practiced a backward hop with a forward twirl, a front hand stand with a tumble and spin, a hip flip, a double dip, a hug that ended in a break, a walk around and turn and twist, patty cake taps with a flick of the wrists. They danced on and on, Pibble almost forgetting that his friends were somewhere outside the pond. Libble saw a faint look of sadness on Pibble's face, and she understood why. She told Pibble that she also felt sad after seeing his friends. Pibble was quite touched by Libble's sincerity.

Hibble and Zibble, hopping around the pool, tried to think of ways to rescue their friend Pibble. They could not think of anything that would get Pibble out of the magical waters. They both sat down, feeling very dejected, on a log near an abandoned beaver dam at the far end of the pond. They stared into space picking out branches from the beaver dam, and they absent-mindedly began throwing the branches over their heads. As they sat on the log thinking, they continued to pick out and toss away more and more branches from the beaver dam. Without realizing it, they picked out and tossed away about one half of the beaver dam. They stood up and were about to hop away when a trickle of water came through the dam and flowed over Hibble's toe. Hibble hopped away and told Zibble how good the water felt on his toe. Zibble stopped and asked Hibble what water he was talking about. Hibble pointed to a trickle of water coming from the abandoned beaver dam. He suddenly realized why his pal Zibble asked the question. They both stood and stared at each other dumbfounded and realized that there was the answer for rescuing their friend Pibble from the pond.

Without a moment's hesitation, Hibble and Zibble hopped back to the beaver dam and began tossing away more and more branches. Some branches were twisted and tangled with other branches, and it took all the strength of Hibble and Zibble to pry them loose. The more branches they tossed away, the more the water flowed. Soon the water increased at a very fast pace. Hibble and Zibble were struggling with one heavy log that seemed to hold the whole dam together. They lifted and pushed and tried with all the strength they could muster, but the flowing water made it more difficult for them. They slid and slipped and fell. Finally, in one last heroic burst of energy, they lifted up this heavy log just long enough for the flowing water to loosen up all the other branches. The water flow increased and pushed through the remaining logs just before Hibble and Zibble dropped the heavy log. A burst of water came crashing through the dam and carried Hibble and Zibble away, and they washed up on a fallen tree.

Pibble and Libble, who were dancing on the lily pads in the pond, didn't notice the water receding until Libble tried to touch an overhanging branch. She had always been able to touch this branch and now when she couldn't reach it, she imagined the wind had lifted it up. There was no wind, and Libble became frightened. She looked around the pond and saw the water level way below the moss covered rocks. She then realized that the magical pond was losing its waters. She was speechless, and she pointed to the shoreline moving her hand up and down trying to attract Pibble. He saw her moving hand and looked in the direction where she was pointing. He saw the water receding, and he realized what was happening. He became very excited because it meant freedom for him. For Libble it meant the destruction of the only world she had ever known. The water poured out in torrents, tearing away every shred of the beaver dam, and widening the gap of the dam.

It didn't take very long before the water poured out of the pond. The gap was now three times the original size. The force of the water literally tore away mounds of earth that once were the sides of the opening of the beaver dam. Libble and Pibble were standing on the muddy bottom of the pond, staring at the gap in the pond. Libble was so frightened that she could hardly speak. Pibble held her hand in a very comforting way. Pibble grasped Libble's hand very firmly and began hopping with her to freedom through the gap to the outside world. Libble stopped at the gap and turned around to take one last look at what once was her world of magical waters and lily pads. It was a horrifying site. Where the magical waters once were, there was nothing but emptiness and mud. The floating lily pads just lay wrinkled in the mud, their stems twisted and misshapen. For a moment, it was a vision of sadness. Libble quickly turned around and began to hop out of her old world into the new world of reality. Hibble and Zibble, seeing their pal Pibble and Libble leaving the pond, began to hop up and down in excitement.

The sun began to set and dusk settled around the forest. It was too late to go to the town of Jibble to the jitterhop dance. Pibble had so much excitement that he only wanted to return home and relax for the evening. Libble looked at Hibble helplessly and said that she had no home. Hibble, Pibble and Zibble responded together that their home would be her home too. Libble was flattered and extremely happy. Now she had three friends, and she had so much to look forward to. They couldn't hop in a triangle now that there were four. So they formed a diamond and hopped home in this fashion. Hibble hopped to the left, Pibble hopped to the front, Zibble hopped to the right, and Libble hopped to the rear. The forest was very dark, but the whispers of the wind led them along the forest path back to the town of Tibble, the home of Hibble, Pibble, Zibble and Libble.

ACKNOWLEDGEMENTS

For each new morning with its light,
For rest and shelter of the night,
For health and food, for love and friends,
For everything thy goodness sends.
~ Ralph Waldo Emerson

L IFE CAN BE an intense grooming process. Each of us has our own set of challenges and our own unique opportunities to learn, grow and enjoy all that life has to offer. We are all teachers and students for each other, and we all produce the learning together. The people we meet along the journey provide us opportunities and experiences to learn, grow, love and evolve.

When I look back on my life, I've had my fair share of ups and downs, and a lot of smooth sailing. I am truly thankful for everything I have experienced because, with each step forward I have learned more about the beauty and mystery of people, life and relationships.

Of all the blessings I've received, the greatest have been my memories with friends and family, and with all the people I have met along the way who have shared time and space in my heart and in my life.

A lifetime is comprised of our experiences, our memories, other people's memories of us, and the legacy that we leave. Realizing how brief life can be, I have a handful of people to whom I want to express my deepest gratitude.

Acknowledgements

First, special thanks to all those who helped make this book possible.

- ❖ My godfather, Hawkwind Soaring
- ❖ My dear friend, Kelly Straeter
- ❖ My dear friend and graphic artist, Michael Cordova
- ❖ My dear friend, David Cordova
- ❖ My virtual uncle, college mentor and dear friend, Mike Maish
- ❖ My dear friend of over 15 years, Sheri Sharman
- ❖ My dear friend, Tracy Jacobsen
- ❖ My dear friend, Ray Bowers, someone I appreciate and respect
- ❖ My dear friend and virtual uncle, Arthur Cranstoun
- ❖ My videographer and friend, Jordan Bergren
- ❖ My Facebook guru and friend, Nick Parsons
- ❖ My editor and writing guru, Mark David Gerson

Next, the extraordinary people who bring so much light into my life.

Marianne Jacqueline Strauss, Mom

I am deeply grateful for the gift of life I was given by my mother. She may have died when I was young, but I will always cherish the memories I do have of her. There is no doubt in my heart and mind that my mother would love me just the way I am and that she would have supported and encouraged me in all my adventures and journeys. I have thought about her nearly every day since the day she died and have always kept a picture of her with me wherever I am. I truly love and appreciate my mom and thank her for watching over me all these years.

Juliette Strauss, Sister

There is only one person who has been with me since the day I was born: my sister, Juliette. There is no doubt that the illness and death of our mom had a lasting impact on both our lives. In our youth, we both faced a lot of challenges that followed us into adulthood. We both moved out on our own at a young age, and we have both grown stronger through our individual trials and tribulations. Through good times and bad, we have always come full circle and grown stronger and closer. I am truly appreciative of her endless love, support and humor, and for keeping me on my toes throughout my life. She has always loved me and accepted me as I am. I love Juliette with all my heart and soul.

Cathrin Strauss, Mom #2

Cathrin came into my life through her marriage to my father. I was the unexpected gift she received as a result of my mother's illness and death. I could not have asked for a more perfect second mother than Cathrin. From the first day we met, she always treated me like I was her own son and continued to touch my life with the wings of an angel. She always did her best to love and inspire me and was the glue that kept my sense of hope alive. Cathrin also passed away too young, but she left behind the beautiful legacy of my sister Amanda, and the memory of her gentle, creative and caring heart. I will always love and appreciate Cathrin.

Amanda Strauss, Sister

When I was 21, I went on a ten-month journey across Australia and New Zealand. On March 10th, 1986, while in Lilydale, Australia, my dad called to tell me that I now had a new sister. Life has never been the same. Amanda has been a barrel of fun ever since she came into my life. From the first time I took her fishing to the gifts of watching her grow up and get married, she has been an incredible sister and someone I love and care for deeply and joyfully. Amanda and I share the same father. Amanda's mother is Cathrin.

Jordan Strauss Ancel, Brother

Jordan is five years younger than I am. We grew up in different households but spent enough time together to feel a brotherly bond of love and respect. No matter how far apart we may have been in distance, he has always shown his love and support. He has an incredibly healthy outlook on life and has an enormous amount of personal courage and inner strength. I definitely have lots of love and gratitude for my brother! Jordan and I share the same father. Jordan's mother, Teresa, is also someone I love and appreciate.

Arthur Strauss, Father

Words can never describe my father. He is one of the most interesting, loving, adventurous people I have ever met. Now 84, he continues to view life with an open heart and an abundance of happiness. He laughs more than anyone I know, and he can find adventure in the joy of world travels or the simplicity of watching a ladybug walk across a flower petal. He gave me and my sisters and brother life, and he has brought a tremendous amount of joy and hope into other people's lives. I truly love and appreciate my dad, and I am forever grateful for the example of health and vitality he has brought into my life.

Donna Strauss, Cousin

My cousin Donna has always held a special place in my heart. She is someone who I truly love and appreciate. I have so many fun memories of our childhood and I am sincerely grateful that we continue to remain close. She has been a wonderful source of enthusiasm and encouragement for completion of this book. I look forward to remaining close and creating new memories.

Michael Cordova, Dear Friend

Mike is one of the most beautiful, loving, caring people to enter into my life. We have built a rock-solid friendship since the day we first met. If there has ever been a person who has been consistently enthusiastic about life and learning, it's Mike. Anyone who has a chance to get to know him will be truly blessed. He is my best friend, and I am truly grateful for the deep, loving friendship we share. His brother, parents and relatives are so close to my heart that they feel like family.

Kelly Straeter, Dear Friend

Kelly is one of the most sincere, generous, beautiful, funny and real people I have ever met. She has a uniquely charming approach to life, and a strong and gentle heart. She has been there for me in so many different ways and has always brought joy, humor, laughter and love into my life. I truly love, respect and appreciate Kelly for the unique gift she has been in my life.

Virginia Straeter, Dear Friend

Beauty comes in packages. Virginia is Kelly Straeter's mother. Very much like Kelly, Virginia is a loving, caring and generous person. She has brought a tremendous amount of love and joy into my life, and has shown up for me in many ways with the open heart of a dear friend and virtual mother. I will always have love and gratitude for Virginia.

Mike Maish, Dear Friend

Mike is another one of the angels in my life. I have no idea where to begin, other than to thank him for his genuine support throughout my life. In more ways than one, Mike saved my life and provided a powerful pillar of support throughout my journey. Mike has tremendous heart and integrity and is a living demonstration of the power of love and forgiveness.

John Rbaugh, Dear Friend

I have known John since my Junior year in College. He has been there for me as a friend is many different ways. During the time of healing from my Hernia surgery he showed up for me each day to make sure I was comfortable. John is a very loving and caring person and always does his best to be there for friends and family. He feels like family to me, and is someone I love and appreciate.

Autumn Riddle, Dear Friend

I met Autumn while I was living in Yuma, Arizona. Autumn is a rare, beautiful and gentle soul with a deep, loving and caring heart. She is far more than a wonderful artist. She is someone who cares deeply about others and is a true blessing to anyone she gets close to. Autumn has touched my heart and my life with kindness and gentleness. I have a deep love and respect for Autumn.

Noah Greathouse, Dear Friend

Noah is one of the most amazing people I know. He came into my life with bouncing enthusiasm and has always been a magnificent friend. His love for adventure and his high personal standards have always set him apart as someone who genuinely appreciates all life has to offer. Noah, his mother Tanya and his father Alphonso feel like family to me. I'm grateful to have them in my life.

Jon Terry, Dear Friend

Jon is the embodiment of personal and social integrity and of living with purpose and gratitude. When he learns something useful and meaningful, he courageously integrates it into his life and shares it with others. When I am asked to think of someone who embraces the truth that we are all connected, and that we are here as teachers and students for each other, I think of Jon. I have the highest level of love and respect for this gentleman because he walks his truth.

Dorothy Steele, Dear Friend

I met Dorothy during my high school years in Telluride. She is the mother of one of my childhood friends. Dorothy has shown up in my life in numerous ways, both as a friend and a virtual mother. She is an incredible role model for health and wellness and has an endless appreciation for people and life. Dorothy has been a tremendous source of encouragement for this book and for my life. She is someone whom I will always love and appreciate.

Kristi Lyn Gall, Dear Friend

Kristi and I have roots going back to our teenage years in Telluride. She has been a consistent friend and an incredible mirror for my thoughts, ideas and emotions. We have a very intuitive connection and have had many parallel life experiences. No matter where each of us is in our lives, we can always count on each other for genuine friendship and support. Kristi is definitely someone that I love and care about and am grateful to have in my life.

Drew Juen, Dear Friend

Drew has been a true and genuine friend. He has shown up during the best and worst of times and has been consistently honest and genuine. He has incredibly strong character and rock-solid integrity. We have been through quite a few life experiences together and have helped each other to learn and grow. I am truly thankful for his friendship. Drew is someone that I appreciate and respect, and love as a brother.

Marcelee Gralapp, Dear Friend

Marcelee is a true angel in my life and in many people's lives. From the day of my hernia surgery and the four months that followed, she took me into her home with open arms so that I could heal physically and emotionally. She is a deeply loving, caring and generous lady with a tremendous amount of heart and compassion. I truly love, appreciate and respect Marcelee.

Shane Bachman, Dear Friend

Shane and I went to High School together. He is my closest friend from that time in my life. We share incredible childhood memories of extreme skiing in Telluride, camping, climbing, hiking, and immersing ourselves in all the fun and excitement that Telluride had to offer during our youth. Shane is someone that I love and appreciate as a brother.

Jonathan Evans, Dear Friend

Jonathan is by far the funniest person I have ever met - funnier than a barrel of monkeys. He is witty and punny, and has an incredible grasp of how to easily relate with others. He quickly warms up to people with his gentle southern accent. Yet he is sharp as a razor. He is a genuine, sincere and loving person and is an instant source of happiness and laughter. Wherever he goes, he leaves a trail of laughter in everyone's hearts. I am truly grateful for our loving friendship.

David Fitzpatrick & Ron Bates, Dear Friends

While living in Yuma, Arizona, I had the good fortune to meet two incredible gentlemen who quickly became dear friends and mentors of the heart and soul. David and Ron have more wisdom than they do years, and their lives are a true testimony to the power of living with intention, heart and integrity. There are many friendships that I cherish in life. My friendship with these two gentlemen is at the top of the list. I truly love, appreciate and respect them.

Michael Weiner, Dear Friend

Michael has been my father's friend longer than I have been alive. He is a pillar of wisdom and practicality and has been an incredible source of encouragement and support. He is someone I look up to for his personal and professional achievements and for his generous and caring heart. He has been a strong role-model in my life, and someone that I appreciate, love and respect.

Hawkwind Soaring, Godfather

When I moved on my own at age sixteen I met a wizard named Hawkwind. I refer to him as my godfather because, from the day I first met him, he has treated me like his own son and has supported me and guided me during my best and worst times. Hawkwind came into my life during a very vulnerable time for me. My mother had passed away. I was living on my own, seeking answers that would make sense of my life. He introduced me to the path of self-awareness and self-discovery. He planted seeds in my mind that allowed me to go through life seeing myself as a spiritual being having a human experience, rather than a human being having a spiritual experience. I am truly grateful for having the gift of a wizard named Hawkwind.

Also, I want to give thanks to these people, all of whom have shown up in a meaningful way — as friends, teachers, guides and/or mentors. Each has left a lasting impression upon my heart and mind.

Amber Waits, Amy Taylor, Anthony Robbins, Ardath Michael, Aron Parker, Bernadette Ramraka, Bill Gouldd, Bill Lewis, Bill Masters, Blake Mallen, Boone Kizer, Brad Sharp, Cam Tyler, Carol Abel, Cheryl Anway, Chris Hendrickson, Christopher Leach, Danny Hirsch, Danny Paige, David Malott, Don Gorsuch, Eddie & Freddie Roufa, Erik Fallenius, George Housney, Gerry Gruber, Gregory Kowalik, Hank Smith, Imo Sharman, Jason Portnoy, Jim Looney, John Napoli, Jackie and Chuck Arguelles, James Evenson, James McCutcheon, James Arthur Ray, Jeff Fountain, Jeff Wheeler, Jessica Robbins, Jim Brand, Jim Lamancusa, Jon Troshynski, Judy DeAngelo, Justin Abrams, Kel Davidson, Kent Bozlinski, Larry Weinstein, Laura Lago, Lee Zeller, Ligia Ramírez, Mark Wiechmann, Matthew Bolin, Micah Page, Michael Beckwith, Mimi Newstadt, Myra Hunter, Nate Auffort, Nels Cary, Norman Squier, Patrick Sofarelli, Peter Garber, Richard Hart, Rick Underwood, Robert Spencer, Robert Woodson, Sandy Sucharski, Stephanie Gebauer, Steve Gumble, Susan Skelton, Tony Zito.

Finally, none of this would have been possible if it hadn't been for that silly rock, to which I owe my deepest debt of gratitude. That rock changed my life. Hopefully, it has changed yours too!

About The Author

The great thing in the world is not so much where we stand, as in what direction we are moving.

~ *Oliver Wendell Holmes*

DAVID STRAUSS has a unique passion for life. He is known for his contagious smile, his forgiving heart, his willingness to listen to and encourage anyone, and his endless enthusiasm for making a positive and lasting difference in the lives of others.

David leads an active life which mirrors his love of health and fitness. He is an outdoor enthusiast and loves being amidst the beauty and solitude of nature. His favorite outdoor activities include hiking, mountaineering, camping, climbing, skiing, snow-shoeing, mountain biking, mountain running, sea-kayaking and SCUBA Diving.

Blending his love for nature and living an active lifestyle, David enjoys using sports, fitness and outdoor activities as vehicles for inspiring others. He is an ISSA Certified Fitness Trainer, Certified Spinning Instructor, Master of Giggle Yoga, International Athlete, and lifetime fitness enthusiast. He enjoys helping people to improve their overall health by introducing them to the importance of eating whole foods and the joy of living an active lifestyle.

As an expression of his love for community, David has been a fund-raising athlete for a variety of organizations, including Meals-On-Wheels, Cancer Research, Boulder Youth Shelter, Multiple Sclerosis Society, Various

Homeless Shelters, the American Diabetes Association, and the American Heart Association. In January of 1995, as a benefit for the University of Colorado Cancer Research Foundation, David and his climbing team reached the 23,000 foot summit of Aconcagua, Argentina, the tallest mountain in the western and southern hemispheres.

In addition to being a fund raising athlete, David has been a Key-Note Graduation Speaker at the Emily Griffith Center for Disadvantaged Youth in Denver, Colorado. He has also volunteered for various community projects in Telluride, including the local radio station – KOTO Telluride.

David is an international traveler, a true Globe-Trotter, with a genuine love for humanity. From bustling cities to remote villages and ancient ruins, and anywhere in between, David always reaches out and makes friends with members of the local community and indigenous peoples.

A graduate of Telluride High School (1983), David earned his BA in Communication at the University of Colorado at Boulder (1990), where he also earned his Colorado Real Estate Broker's License.

He counts among his accomplishments being a graduate of Anthony Robbins Mastery University as well as having been a 2nd Lieutenant in the US Air Force Auxiliary. Through his involvement in the National Character and Leadership Symposium *and* The Center for Leadership and Character Development at the United States Air Force Academy, David has added to his broad range of personal and professional resources.

From his High School days until today, through international travel, and a strong commitment to personal development and community service, David has developed a deep insight into human nature, a strong respect for the diversity of humanity, and a genuine appreciation for the gift of life.

Recommended Readings

A book is the only place in which you can examine a fragile thought without breaking it, or explore an explosive idea without fear it will go off in your face. It is one of the few havens remaining where a man's mind can get both provocation and privacy.
~ Edward P. Morgan

Allen, James. *As a man thinketh* . Running Press miniature ed. Philadelphia, Pa.: Running Press, 2001 1989. Print.

Haggai, John Edmund. *Paul J. Meyer and the art of giving* . Atlanta, Ga.: Kobrey Press, 1994. Print.

Hill, Napoleon. *Think and grow rich* . New and rev. ed. No. Hollywood, Calif.: Melvin Powers, Wilshire Book Co., 1966. Print.

Maltz, Maxwell. *Psycho-cybernetics* . New York: Pocket Books, 1969 1960. Print.

Mandino, Og.. *The greatest miracle in the world* . New York: Bantam, 1975 1977. Print.

Mandino, Og.. *The greatest secret in the world: featuring your own success recorder diary with the ten great scrolls for success from The greatest salesman in the world*. Bantam ed. New York: Bantam Books, 1978 1972. Print.

Mandino, Og., and Buddy Kaye. *The gift of Acabar* . New York: Bantam Book, 1979 1978. Print.

Mandino, Og.. *The greatest success in the world* . New York: Bantam Books, 1982 1981. Print.

Mandino, Og.. *A Better Way To Live* . Toronto: Bantam Books, 1990. Print.

Mandino, Og.. *The greatest salesman in the world* . New York: Bantam, 1991 1968. Print.

Mandino, Og.. *The greatest miracle in the world* . Bantam ed. New York: Bantam Books, 19971975. Print.

Millman, Dan. *Way of the peaceful warrior: a book that changes lives.* New rev. ed. Tiburon, Calif.: H.J. Kramer ;, 2000. Print.

Millman, Dan. *The journeys of Socrates: an adventure.* San Francisco: HarperSanFrancisco, 2006 2005. Print.

Peale, Norman Vincent. *The power of positive thinking* . New York: Fawcett Crest, 1991 1956. Print.

Proctor, Bob. *You were born rich: now you can discover and develop those riches.* Cartersville, Ga.: LifeSuccess Productions, 1997. Print.

Ralston, Aron. *Between a rock and a hard place* . New York: Atria Books, 2005 2004. Print.

Robbins, Anthony. *Unlimited power: the new science of personal achievement.* New York : Simon & Schuster, 1997. Print.

Ruiz, Miguel. *The four agreements: a practical guide to personal freedom.* San Rafael, Calif.: Amber-Allen Pub., 1997. Print.

Ruiz, Miguel. *The mastery of love: a practical guide to the art of relationship.* San Rafael, Calif.: Amber-Allen Pub., 1999. Print.

Tolle, Eckhart. *The Power Of Now: A Guide To Spiritual Enlightenment* . Vancouver: Namaste Publishing Inc., 1999. Print.

Yogananda, Paramahansa. *Autobiography of a Yogi* . 12th ed. Los Angeles, Calif.: Self-Realization Fellowship, 1993 1981. Print.

— Excerpts —

Footsteps After The Fall

"**When the universe gives you a near-death experience,** your entire perception of life changes, and you come out with a deep appreciation for life that can only be seen through the eyes of someone who has faced death."

"**The only things we ever have to hold onto** are the things we are afraid to let go of."

"**We are the traveler and the trail,** the seeker and the teacher. The experiences of life are the classroom, our thoughts are our map, and our heart is our guidance system."

"**There is no greater experience** in the world than to fall in love with our own life. Once we find the love that we seek within our own hearts, then the love that we find in own heart can be found in anyone's heart."

"**When one door appears to close,** it is only because that experience no longer serves our higher good and it has given us a sign that we are ready to move in a different direction in life."

"**Let the past be free.** Garden your heart and mind. Pull out the weeds of fear, poverty, lack and limitation, and plant the seeds of your dreams — seeds of love, health, happiness, community, family, cooperation and endless prosperity.

"**Everything we seek** — peace, love, laughter, happiness, abundance, understanding — can be found within us and amongst us."

LaVergne, TN USA
30 January 2011
214532LV00003B/5/P